MORE CASES OF A PRIVATE EYE

This second book of Ernest Dudley's stories about his London-based private eye character, Nat Craig, finds Craig's clients making up a pretty varied collection. Young, wealthy women getting themselves blackmailed; wealthier men or women who have the jitters over the safety of their precious family heirlooms; occasionally even members of the ex-crook class, appeal to him for help. And not infrequently Craig finds himself confronted with grisly murders, testing his tough resourcefulness and considerable powers of deduction.

Classic British crime stories with an intriguing psychological slant on characters from every walk of life!

ERNEST DUDLEY

MORE CASES OF A PRIVATE EYE

LINFORD
Leicester

First published in Great Britain

First Linford Edition
published 2014

*A catalogue record for this book is available
from the British Library.*

ISBN 978–1–4448–1905–2

Published by
F. A. Thorpe (Publishing)
Anstey, Leicestershire

Set by Words & Graphics Ltd.
Anstey, Leicestershire
Printed and bound in Great Britain by
T. J. International Ltd., Padstow, Cornwall

This book is printed on acid-free paper

1

The Redhead Murder

Babs Wilson had never had much of a break. Until she met Ken Morris. Not that he was much to look at, with his sparse black hair topping a sallow-complexioned face and thin stooping shoulders.

It was the stoop that added years to his age, though he was a good deal older than Babs for a start. Still, Ken had what it takes — money. It was a necessary item to Babs's way of living and if it meant taking Ken along with it, Babs could do that too.

'I like Ken,' she would protest to critical friends, smoothing back her long straight hair that flamed like fire. 'And anyway, I've had to scrimp along on my own for long enough. I'm sick to hell of living in a one-eyed back room in the Fulham Road.'

So, for a year, she had what she wanted. She exchanged the back room for a

1

modern flat of her own and the Fulham Road for Mayfair. She had clothes to match the flat and jewellery to match the clothes and Ken Morris was easy to manage.

She didn't quite know when Ken first ceased to be so easy.

The change took place gradually and she hardly noticed when he began taking her to less expensive restaurants. Then one day, he told her she would have to move to a less expensive neighbourhood.

Babs sat up then.

'But why, Ken?' she asked sulkily, wondering whether it would be worth-while mussing up her make-up by trying to produce a tear or two. 'Isn't business good any more?'

She had never had a very clear idea of what Ken's business was. So long as the cash came rolling in it was enough and she was not curious. Now, apparently the cash wasn't rolling. She began wondering about his suite of luxurious offices, ostensibly there for the comfort of his clients wishing for advice on the interior decoration of their homes.

'It's Lucas,' he said morosely.

Babs remembered.

A few months ago he had taken a partner and the firm had become Morris and Lucas. She had only met Lucas once, and then he had been bouncy and very ready to allow Ken to buy the drinks.

She asked:

'What's the matter with him?'

He fidgeted and looked uncomfortable.

'He's difficult,' he said evasively.

Babs hunched a slim shoulder and her flecked green eyes grew cold.

'Then get rid of him.'

Ken said miserably:

'I can't. You don't understand, Babs.'

Babs didn't. She didn't understand what had come over Ken at all. In his quiet, shifty way he had up til then always been so successful. But she was going to find out. She visited Lucas the following morning at a time when she knew Ken wouldn't be there. Lucas wasn't so shy about telling her one or two things in connection with the luxurious suite of offices that Ken had not thought necessary to impart to her.

'You mean,' Babs said incredulously, 'all this is a cover-up for receiving stolen goods?'

Lucas smiled unpleasantly.

'Just that.'

'And Ken doesn't know a thing about interior decorating?'

Lucas shrugged.

'Not very much, my dear.'

Babs was quiet for a bit, and she didn't register a thing.

But Lucas, watching her, knew that she was doing some pretty rapid thinking. At last she said shrewdly:

'What do you get out of this?'

Lucas was still smiling as he spread out his hands.

''Bout half the profits, naturally.'

'And?'

'I don't understand you. Ken and I are very good friends — '

Babs thought back. It was ever since Lucas had become a partner that her profits had ceased to be so profitable.

'You're blackmailing him,' she said flatly. Little devils of fury were dancing in her eyes.

4

Lucas cocked his head on one side. He said softly:

'You're very astute, my dear.'

She went on quickly:

'I could go to the police about you both, or — '

'Or blackmail us both?' Lucas laughed loudly. 'You wouldn't be such a fool.' He leaned forward in genuine amusement. 'I get half the profits — on the interior decorating. That's perfectly legal. If the police got on to some unpleasant facts about Ken — well, I wouldn't know anything about that side of his life, would I? I should, of course, be very shocked.'

'You swine,' she said between her teeth.

Suddenly she relaxed. Her brain was working quickly. If Lucas had put one over on Ken, Lucas would be the one with the money. She smiled suddenly.

'And,' Lucas said urbanely, watching her out of his creased-up little eyes, 'I'm not quite so susceptible as Ken, my dear.'

She knew what he meant but she wasn't going to give up so easily. Lucas might feel differently after she'd got to work on him. If he didn't, she'd think of something else. But one thing she did know, and that was that she wasn't going to lose what she'd got. Not after all those long years of waiting and doing without.

'I know,' she agreed submissively. 'You're clever. But I must talk to Ken. Will you meet me tonight?'

Lucas went on smiling.

'I don't mind buying you a drink, if Ken doesn't,' he told her. 'But it won't do you any good.'

She said, 'I'd like a longer talk with you, that's all. I have to go now.'

★   ★   ★

Although it was early, the Mirrobar was crowded. Craig steered Simone expertly to the bar and ordered two whiskies.

'You'll feel better when you get outside that,' he told her. 'Here's to crime.'

They had dropped in for a drink before he took her out to dinner at a little place he knew. She had a yearning for somewhere quiet and cosy.

Craig took a swift look round the bar. There was no one he wanted to know and he was just about to return his entire attention to Simone, when his glance was arrested by a girl sitting at a table in the corner. She was talking to a man who had his back to Craig.

Simone broke off saying something and her eyes followed Craig's. She frowned.

'She's pretty, in a hard way.'

Craig laughed.

'Allergic to redheads?'

But Simone was right. The girl was attractive and showing plenty of sheer silk-stocking. Her hair was beautiful. Like a flame, and long and silky.

Craig worked his gaze round to her face and it startled him.

There was a murderous look about the sulky mouth. He switched over to her companion. There was something vaguely familiar about his back. The thick square-ness of the neck and shoulders.

Craig frowned over the flame of his lighter. His narrowed eyes went on puzzling about the identity of that back.

Quite suddenly the redhead stood up. It was a swift movement, like a python preparing to strike, and she seemed to be issuing an ultimatum.

The man leaned back and laughed, then he shook his head The redhead bent over the table, her long hair falling over the curve of her cheek and, from the fierce way she was speaking, Craig gathered the conversation was not exactly dripping with friendship. The man made a short reply and the redhead mashed her cigarette angrily into an ashtray and without another word stormed across to the door.

As she went the man turned, obviously amused, to witness her exit, and in a flash Craig got it.

'What is it?' Simone asked him.

Craig unhitched himself from the bar.

'Hang on a second,' he told her, 'and keep your eye on that character in the corner with the neck like a bull. I'll be back.'

'But — '

But Craig wasn't there any more. He reached the door only just in time to spot the redhead standing on the kerb outside. She was clearly waiting for someone.

As Craig hesitated in the doorway, a

thin little figure of a man joined her under the street lamp; they exchanged a few words and then the girl hailed a cruising cab. Craig was too far away to catch the address. Then, as he didn't want to lose his old friend in the bar, he made his way back to Simone.

'The man in the corner has just left by the other door,' she told him. She was tapping an impatient foot. Her curiosity got the better of her. 'Who was he?'

'He's an unsavoury customer by the name of Lucas. He's been mixed up in every kind of racket you can think of plus a few more. So far he has managed to evade the police. Last I heard he'd been abroad. Wonder what the game is this time.'

'Maybe he's gone and got straight ideas?' suggested Simone.

'So has a spiral staircase.'

They had another drink. Craig downed it in silence. Out of the blue he announced:

'I'm slipping.'

'Why?' asked Simone, not visibly perturbed.

He looked at her.

'Lucas. We might do some checking up.'

'He's been gone a long time.'

'We'll take a chance and call on him.'

'I thought he had been abroad?'

Craig was piloting her to the door.

'So he has. But he has a house in Kensington, which he may have returned to. It's worth a try.'

Simone said nothing. There seemed to be nothing to say. After all, she liked excitement, in or out of office hours.

Five minutes later they turned into Park Lane and grabbed a taxi. A quarter of an hour later they drew up outside a large house surrounded by a beshrubbed garden in an expensive corner of Kensington. There was a light burning in a downstairs room.

'There's someone in, anyway,' Simone murmured as Craig turned from paying off the driver.

'Question is — who?' Craig smiled at her in the darkness.

He rang twice before the door opened a crack and a sallow-faced individual poked his nose into the air.

'What's the matter?' Craig asked with concern. 'Afraid of getting a cold?'

'What do you want?'

'To see Mr. Lucas.'

'I'm afraid — ' began Sallow Face, then he glanced down at Craig's feet neatly wedged between door and doorpost and licked his lips. 'Perhaps you had better come in.'

'That's what I thought,' Craig said chattily.

Standing under the hall light, the man peered at them nervously and fingered his lapel.

'I'm afraid — ' he tried again.

'We gathered you are.' Craig was finding the conversation beginning to sag. 'If Mr. Lucas isn't in, we'll wait.'

For a second something like a sour smile appeared round Sallow Face's lips, but it was a fleeting expression. Then he lowered his eyes and said primly:

'He is in.'

'What are we waiting for?'

'He's dead.'

Sallow Face's reply was something

Craig hadn't expected. He snapped:

'Where is he?'

'Upstairs.' The other took a flickering look at Craig's face as he placed his hand on the banister. 'It — it is a terrible tragedy. I think he's been murdered. You must forgive me if I seem — ' He broke off. 'I'm rather upset. I have just telephoned the police.'

'That's something,' Craig said. 'Come on. Show me the way.'

Simone made a move to follow him. He admired her determination but there was no need for her to get mixed up in this more than was necessary. 'Keep guard in the hall,' he told her.

She nodded and drifted obediently back to the front door.

Sallow Face was waiting patiently on the bottom stair. 'You are a friend of Mr. Lucas?'

'Yes,' Craig said without hesitation. 'You?'

The man stared into space.

'I was his partner,' he replied quietly. 'My name is Morris. Ken Morris.'

Partner in what, Craig wondered. But

12

he said nothing and padded up the stairs behind the other.

Before a closed door, Morris stopped.

'It's not so very nice,' he said.

Craig looked at him curiously. The man obviously was upset. He didn't look as if he had the guts to kill a mouse. Craig decided at this stage to keep an open mind.

'I don't suppose it is. Let's go in.'

Without another word Morris opened the door and stepped into the room. Lucas was sprawled untidily across the bed, blood oozing from the dent in his head. A newspaper on a chair flapped dismally in the light breeze that drifted through the open window.

Craig paused for a moment by the bed and then walked over to the window. Morris watched him silently from the door.

'What do you know?' Craig asked over his shoulder.

'Not very much. I was downstairs. Mr. Lucas had come up here to fetch some papers he wanted to show me, when I heard the scream. I came as fast as I could but

13

when I arrived I found him like this.'

'Was the window open?'

'I was coming to that.'

Morris's mouth twitched with nerves and emotion. Craig let him talk.

'When I recovered from the first shock I went over to the window and looked out. There was a man climbing over the wall in the back garden — too dark to see properly. He — he must have descended the ladder that is against the window sill.'

Craig smiled thinly.

'I had noticed it. Were you two alone in the house?'

'Yes. There is a manservant but he is away on holiday.'

Craig shrugged.

'Not much more we can do until the police arrive.'

He followed Morris down into the hall.

Simone was waiting by the front door wearing a martyred look. Craig grinned at her.

'We'll wait in there,' he said to Morris, indicating a door on the right. By his reckoning it must be the room where they had seen a light earlier.

'You are going to wait?'

There was a surprised lift to the man's dreary tones.

Craig's eyebrows lifted.

'Naturally. The police will want to see us, astonishing as it may seem to you.'

Morris permitted himself to smile.

'Very well.'

He opened the door into the lounge. It was a long room, running the width of the house with windows back and front. Craig wandered thoughtfully over to the window that led into the back garden.

'Check up on that phone call,' he told Simone.

Morris sat himself quietly down in an unobtrusive corner while she picked up the receiver and dialled. When she had hung up she went over to Craig.

'They're on their way,' she told him as he lit a cigarette. 'Incidentally, I thought I heard someone moving about in here while I was waiting in the hall.'

Craig threw a glance over in Morris's direction. He did not appear to have heard them.

'It wouldn't altogether surprise me,'

Craig murmured. He stepped through the French windows that led on to the gravel path running round the house.

His eyes flicked over the loose earth at the base of the thirty-foot ladder that stood about two feet away from the foundations of the house. The ladder reached up to the window of Lucas's bedroom. He smiled grimly as he stooped down to inspect more closely the prints of a man's shoes in the soft ground.

When he was through he went back into the lounge and said to Morris:

'Is there any other way out of the back garden except through this room?'

'No. There is no connecting path through to the front garden, and, as you can see, a wall surrounds the back.'

There was a hush in the room as Craig tapped the ash off his cigarette into the grate in a leisurely fashion.

'That's what I thought.'

He said it so softly that the hidden meaning in his words temporarily escaped Morris.

'The man I saw escaping over the wall must have had a grudge against poor

Lucas,' Morris said expressionlessly. 'I — I don't like to say it, but Lucas had a funny way with him. Of course, he and I always got on extremely well,' he added hastily. 'But there is no denying it, Lucas had got enemies.'

A crafty glint had appeared in Morris's eyes. He moved in a sliding movement and stood at Craig's shoulder looking up at him.

'By the way,' he inquired softly, 'who are you?'

'Craig,' said Craig. He didn't see why, at this juncture, he should enlighten him any further.

Morris puzzled over the name.

'Sounds familiar. Why so officious, checking up on my phone calls?'

'I'm a friend of Lucas.' There was no mistaking the mockery in Craig's tone. 'As good a friend as you were.'

'Maybe I heard Lucas say something about you.' Then another angle occurred to him. 'What do you mean, as good a friend as I was?'

Craig looked innocent.

'Weren't you?'

'Yes, I was. I told you that.' The crafty look had returned to his eyes. 'Maybe we have a lot in common.'

Craig shook his head.

'I don't really care for redheads,' he said chattily. 'I go for brunettes.'

'What do you mean?'

'You should know what I mean by redheads. By the way, where is she?'

'Where is who?'

Craig sighed.

'What a lot of question and answer we do have before we get anywhere. The girlfriend. *Your* girlfriend. Strawberry-blonde, I believe is another name for 'em — and this one has a temper. You'll have to be careful!'

'Careful?'

'Here we go again. Yes, careful. You might go the same way as Lucas. Anyway, I'm crazy to meet her and she was here a few minutes ago.'

He looked round with interest.

Simone's eyes widened as the other backed against a small table.

'I don't know what your game is, Mr. Craig, or who you are, but I do know you know too much.' He leapt for Craig's throat, but he never reached it: he was much too busy sprawling backwards against the table after he had collided head-on with a punch like a kangaroo's kick. As he staggered to his feet:

'Good night, Mr. Morris.' That was the last he heard before something like a block of steel hit him somewhere on the point of the chin and he slid into a deep and peaceful sleep.

Craig turned to Simone.

'It's so easy — ' he began, but she wasn't there.

Over by the open window the redhead was raising herself slowly and painfully from a position she had been occupying flat on her face on the carpet. Over her stood a breathless but triumphant Simone, clutching a poker in one hand. She looked at Craig.

'You were saying?' she asked.

He grinned at her. He said:

'Just that it's easy when you know how. And apparently you know how. What happened?'

'Just as that horrible man jumped at

you I saw the curtain by the window move. You were busy so I thought I would do a little work myself. So, when she came out with a poker in her hand I kicked her hard on the shin and tripped her up.'

Craig started to laugh. He cast a dispassionate eye on the redhead.

'Get up,' he told her. 'You look much more alluring on your feet.'

She paid no attention but continued to sit on the floor, her head in her hands with her red hair falling about her face.

'Get up.'

She looked at him, her green eyes dazed, but there was all fury there too.

'What the hell do you think you're doing?' she demanded.

'I might,' said Craig politely, 'ask you the same.'

'Mind your own business.'

Craig shrugged.

'Have it your way. Only the police will be here in a minute and they will probably want to know. If they don't already.'

'They don't. I'm Babs Wilson.' Her lip curled. 'If that's any use to you.'

He smiled blandly.

She scrambled to her feet, glowering at him. Craig said chattily, 'I've got all the information we'll need but I'd like to know why you did it.'

'Did — what?'

'Murdered Lucas.'

He lit a cigarette and eyed her over the top of his lighter. She had gone deathly white and her hand pushing her hair back was shaking.

'I didn't,' she whispered. Suddenly she began screaming. 'I didn't. I didn't. I swear I didn't do it — it was Ken.'

She started to sob.

Craig eyed her for a second or two.

'Maybe you didn't sock him the fatal blow,' he allowed. 'But your boyfriend Morris would never have done it if you hadn't planned the thing. You certainly weren't friendly with Lucas.'

'How do you know?'

Craig smiled again.

'You shouldn't have such obvious quarrels with men like Lucas in public places.'

Her attitude changed.

'They can't do anything to me. It was

Ken, I tell you. Ken Morris. Lucas was blackmailing him. I tried to persuade Lucas to lay off. He — he just laughed at me. He deserved all he got.'

Her eyes held that murderous quality that he had noticed in the Mirrobar.

'I could agree with you on that,' Craig said, 'but unfortunately for you, it is still murder. Ken Morris wouldn't have had the guts to carry it out unless you were on the premises to see that he did. He had been paying blackmail money to Lucas quite meekly until you discovered it,' he hazarded shrewdly. 'It was bad luck we turned up before you could make your getaway as you had planned to do. And it was bad luck my secretary stayed in the hall barring your only exit. Pity for you that you didn't know then it was only a girl out there or you might have chanced it.'

Her choked reply was drowned by a shrill ringing at the doorbell. Craig nodded to Simone.

'Let them in. It's the police.'

She started across the room then stopped.

'How did you get on to Morris and her?' she asked curiously.

Craig grinned. 'When Morris stood under the hall light I recognized him as the man under the street lamp, which tied him up with her. That started me thinking. I knew later that it couldn't be the outside job they wanted it to appear to be.'

'How?'

'It was the ladder. It stood two feet away from the wall of the house. Anyone trying to climb a thirty-foot ladder in that position would have upset its centre of gravity and the ladder would have tipped backwards.'

The ringing outside started up again.

'The law,' he added, 'is getting impatient.'

Simone smiled at him. 'I will let them in,' she said, and went out into the hall.

2

The Millionaire's Daughter

Burton Malone's millions had been acquired because a junior public all over the world held a passion for fizzy drinks, and the fizzy drinks which they guzzled through straws always went over much bigger if they had Burton Malone's name plastered on the bottles.

He'd had three wives. One son by his first wife and a daughter by the third. The boy had been as disappointing as his mother and had ended a hectic and dissipated career by being smashed to pieces in a car accident after a party at which his father's fizzy drinks had not been a speciality.

His daughter Claire was a lovely girl. All the society magazines said so, so did the dress-designers and the newspapers. The really astonishing thing about Claire Malone was the fact that she was also a charming girl and a dutiful daughter. Her father used to say only two things in his life had been worthwhile: his fizzy drinks because they enabled him to indulge in the luxury he loved, and his daughter Claire whom he idolized.

So when Claire went and got herself engaged to Rozzani the famous violinist, her father, who up to this date had never had much time for music and less for musicians, became a fervent admirer of Rozzani's.

Craig, who never drank fizzy drinks but liked the pictures of Claire, knew a few things about the private life of the millionaire though he'd never seen him. That is, until one day when Simone came in and told him there was a client waiting in the outer office.

'Who?' inquired Craig laconically without taking his feet off the desk.

'Burton Malone.'

Craig raised an eyebrow.

'He hasn't got himself a fourth wife he doesn't want has he?'

She shrugged.

'Not that I know of.'

'Somebody's suing him for hiccups caused by too much gas in the fizz?'

She shrugged again. It was a pretty shrug. Craig liked it.

'I don't think so.'

'Then I'll see him,' Craig said, 'and my fees will be extortionate.'

Burton Malone was ushered into the inner sanctum and came to the point pronto.

'The job I have in mind for you, Mr. Craig, may seem a little strange I'm afraid, but my daughter needs your help.'

He said it as if that would explain everything.

Craig gazed at him quizzically through a cloud of cigarette smoke and said what he had said so many times before he was thinking of having a record made of it.

'I'm a private detective, Mr. Malone. Nothing has struck me as strange these last many moons.'

Burton Malone leaned more comfortably back in his chair and eased up his pinstripe trousers. His rather hard-bitten expression was somehow not in harmony with his immaculate dress. Craig mentally decided Claire must take after her mother.

'As I'm sure you have read,' began the millionaire with a certain satisfaction, 'my daughter Claire is to be married to Rozzani — ' He tilted forward. 'The violinist. Have you heard him play, Mr. Craig? No? He is magnificent, magnificent. But tonight he is making his début at the Albert Hall, and that, I think you will agree, is an important occasion.'

Craig said he would agree it was.

'My daughter,' the other continued with pride, 'was to have been there, naturally.'

'I read it. Very touching story — but you said 'Was'?'

Burton Malone nodded.

'That, Mr. Craig, is the crux of the whole matter. Rozzani worships Claire — who doesn't? And they are very much in love.' The hard expression softened. 'And he will be terribly upset if she is not there.'

'What's the matter? Has she got another date?'

Burton Malone, who had no sense of humour, was shocked. 'I told you they

27

were very much in love. Claire had a nasty fall from her horse in the Row this morning. Don't alarm yourself, it is nothing serious. But enough to keep her in bed for a few weeks.'

Craig obligingly was not alarmed. 'I'm so glad,' he murmured.

'What is worrying her is she will not be able to attend the concert tonight and the effect it will have on Rozzani.'

'He doesn't know about the accident?'

Burton Malone absent-mindedly helped himself to one of Craig's cigarettes.

'No. We've managed to keep it from him,' he replied, fumbling with his lighter.

'Here.'

Craig leant forward, applying the necessary flame. The fizzy drink mogul cleared his throat and went on.

'Thanks. As I was saying, we have so far managed to keep it from him. He is rehearsing all day and won't be seeing her before the concert. But if my daughter is not in her box tonight he will realize something is wrong.'

Craig asked:

'And that would be bad?' He was

enjoying himself.

'Very bad, Mr. Craig,' the other answered seriously. 'He relies on my daughter being there to get him through the concert.'

'Then hadn't you better explain what's happened before he is really disappointed?'

Burton Malone shook his head.

'He would be frantic with worry. He wouldn't be able to play a note.'

'A temperamental cuss,' observed Craig.

'That — and he is mad about Claire.'

Craig eyed him with foreboding. 'And I thought of fourth wives and hiccups,' he said. 'I imagined I'd covered everything.'

'Eh?'

Craig let it ride. He said: 'The gag couldn't be, I suppose, that you want me to impersonate your daughter tonight? Female impersonation isn't exactly in my line, in or out of the Albert Hall.'

Burton Malone didn't laugh, but Craig hadn't hoped he would.

'Rozzani happens to be short-sighted — ' he said. He continued: 'I imagine you could find a young woman who could impersonate my daughter sufficiently to fool him during the performance. The platform is some distance away from the box and if your girl wore a dress belonging to Claire and did her hair in the same way I'm sure she'd get away with it.'

'I'll have my chorus out immediately so that you can take your pick.'

Burton Malone frowned.

'I'm perfectly serious, Mr. Craig.'

'Is it really all that important? You really believe all this is necessary?'

Burton Malone assumed the look of somebody whose every whim was always important, no matter what.

'I wouldn't be taking up your time, or mine, Mr. Craig, if I didn't think so.'

'Have it your way.' Craig was beginning to feel long-suffering. 'Rozzani will know about it afterwards?'

'So long as he gets through the performance we don't have to worry about the afterwards. My daughter and Rozzani will have been saved a great deal of anxiety. There is a picture of Claire.'

His hand went to his breast pocket and reverently drew forth a studio portrait.

Craig glanced at it, saying:

'I'm afraid I can't offer you much choice.'

He rang for Simone. As she entered and turned an inquiring glance on him, he asked:

'Will she do?'

Burton Malone looked.

'Couldn't be better,' he approved at once.

Craig grinned.

'Have you heard of Rozzani?' he asked Simone.

'The violinist?'

'You're going to hear him tonight.'

She smiled uncertainly and managed to look intrigued and surprised simultaneously and Craig thought the total result entrancing.

'But it would be lovely.' She looked hopefully at Craig. 'And you will be coming too?'

'Not me,' he smiled. 'Mr. Malone is treating you. You'll be in his box.'

'Huh?'

'Actually,' said Craig carefully, 'you'll be wearing his daughter's dress and hair style and you will be impersonating her.'

'Will I? But, why?'

Briefly Craig outlined the way things were and ended tactfully:

'Claire Malone is extremely pretty so you have only to be yourself and you're in.'

'Thank you.'

'There's no danger,' he said sweetly.

Burton Malone rose from his chair.

'Well, that's settled then. I shall be going to the concert direct from my office, but if this young lady will be at my house this evening, my daughter's maid will fix her up and my car will take her to the Albert Hall.'

'Nice for you,' said Craig when he had gone. Simone had made her way over to the window.

'I wonder if that's the car I shall have,' she said dreamily. 'It's huge.'

Craig glanced over her shoulder in time to see the chauffeur open the door for Burton Malone and tuck a rug round his knees.

'Looks like you're booked for an amusing evening. Even the chauffeur's a good-looking character.'

⋆　⋆　⋆

Their taxi pulled up outside the Regency house just behind Park Lane at four thirty.

'It gives me masses of time,' Simone remarked as Craig saw her up the steps.

Back on the pavement again he noticed Burton Malone's big dark limousine pulled up by the kerb with the chauffeur behind the wheel. Without pausing he drew out his cigarette case and fumbled for his lighter. Then he stopped and walked up to the waiting car.

'Help me out with a light?' he asked pleasantly. 'My lighter's had it.'

The man grunted something and struck a match.

'Thanks,' said Craig and moved off.

⋆　⋆　⋆

Simone, up in a bedroom that was two shades of pink from top to bottom with white muslin hangings and thick white rugs on the polished parquet flooring, was being fussed over by Claire's maid.

'Miss Claire had a new white dress for

33

tonight. It is wonderful. And it will suit you a treat.'

'Poor Miss Malone. She probably hates the idea of me wearing her dress and going to the concert.'

'Oh, no, Miss. She'd hate it a lot more if she thought Mr. Rozzani was going to worry.'

Simone looked at herself in the mirror. 'I think,' she murmured, 'I ought always to have the opportunity of dressing in white crêpe.'

The maid, her head on one side, raved:

'Miss, it's beautiful. It looks like it was made for you.'

Apparently Claire Malone had been going to wear her hair on top of her head and the maid dutifully went to work on Simone.

'It's funny,' the girl exclaimed when she had finished and Simone was clipping on the diamond earrings, 'you do really look like Miss Claire.'

'I hope Mr. Rozzani will think so too.'

Simone caught up the fur cape lying on the bed. 'Now for it.'

'Good luck, Miss. You do look lovely

— and I do hope you have a beautiful evening. Mr. Rozzani plays ever so nice, I've heard.'

Going down the stairs, Simone wished privately that Craig was going to be there too.

The waiting chauffeur touched his cap and held the door open for her. So he hadn't noticed that she was not Miss Claire Malone. Simone mentally patted herself on the back at her initial success.

He slammed the door quickly. So quickly in fact, that she was flung back into the corner as the car lurched forward with a purr of its muted engine.

It was then she realized with a cold little shock that she was not alone.

The man beside her said softly:

'Good evening, Miss Malone.'

'Who are you?'

She tried to get a better look at him in the gloom. His overcoat collar was turned up to his ears and his slouch hat pulled down well over his face. All she could see of his features were his glittering eyes and the curve of a lean cheek; the rest was lost in shadow.

'Who are you?' she asked again, panic rising, but telling herself not to be a fool at the same time.

He reached out a gloved hand and took her arm in a grip that hurt.

'Take it easy,' he said, 'and everything will be all right.'

The awful feeling of panic was climbing so that she felt sick with it. Her throat was frighteningly tight and dry, but she managed to keep her voice steady.

'What do you mean — everything will be all right?'

The voice that answered her in the darkness mocked her.

'What I say, Miss Malone. You be a good girl and no harm will come to you.'

'Harm?'

'This is a snatch job,' he told her succinctly, brutally. 'Your father will pay up for your safety.'

With a terrific wrench Simone tore herself free of his grasp and leaned forward beating wildly on the glass partition.

He seized her shoulder and pulled her roughly back into her corner.

'That won't do you any good. The

driver is in on this too.'

Simone tried desperately to think what Craig would do.

'But I've got to be at the Albert Hall, You don't understand — '

The other only laughed.

Craig. If only Craig had been there he would — he would — what? He would light a cigarette and shrug his shoulders, and she could almost hear him say: 'Have it your way, son. I never liked music much either.' She held out an imperious little hand. 'I'd like a cigarette, please,' she said as calmly as she could. But her French accent was very pronounced. The man obliged and as he struck a match, Simone added, 'But you have made one big mistake. I am not Claire Malone.'

'You're a cool — ' he started and then broke off and brought the match nearer to her face so that the flame almost scorched her cheek. 'No, my God, you're not!' he exclaimed. 'I thought there was something funny about your voice — foreign.'

'French.'

Simone, congratulating herself she was putting it over in quite the Craig manner, said: 'I am Simone Thérése Marie Antoinette Lamont. You can settle for Simone,' she said. Her courage was coming back fast.

The man muttered, 'What the hell is all this?'

Simone retorted:

'You tell me.'

'What the hell — ?' But this time the other wasn't worrying over the problem of Simone. The car was squealing to a standstill. Simone peered out.

They were in one of the quiet back streets near Shepherds Market and ahead of them two cars were pulling across the road, blocking their route. The big limousine stopped and suddenly shot into reverse, throwing Simone and her companion almost on to their knees. The man scrambled up and took a lightning glance out of the back window.

'Eddie,' he shrieked. '*Eddie*. For Pete's sake watch out — there's another one behind us!'

The driver must have caught a glimpse of the police car behind because before the words were out he skidded his car violently up on to the pavement.

'Cops!'

The man made a dive for the door. Simone put out her foot and sent him sprawling into the road. Half out of the door, she saw Eddie run hell for leather straight into the arms of half a dozen figures emerging from the two cars in front. Her late companion was being lugged roughly to his feet by two more figures from the car behind. Then a familiar voice drawled in her ear.

'I might have known you would have been in the thick of it with your famous trip-gag.'

She spun round just as Craig touched her shoulder and looked up into his smiling face.

'You all right?' he asked.

'I'm all right. But how — ?'

'No questions,' he said as he ducked into the driver's seat. 'Looks like our client not only wanted somebody to impersonate his daughter but his chauffeur as well.' Then as Simone slammed the door, he yelled through the glass partition, 'Albert Hall, madam?'

The car mounted further onto the pavement and shot hair-raisingly backwards between the railings of an alley and the stationary police car.

They spun through the London streets as though they were speeding on the Great West Road.

'Well,' Simone remarked shakily as she climbed down outside the Albert Hall. 'I do not know which was worse. Being kidnapped or driven by you.'

He laughed.

'Depends' he said, 'on whether you find Slouch-Hat more attractive or — me? Anyway, we're on time.'

Ten minutes later Craig and Burton Malone slipped out of Simone's box.

'Now I've seen everything is all right,' Burton Malone said, mopping his brow. 'I want a breath of air. Rozzani certainly thinks it's Claire in there, did you see him look up and smile?'

There was a touch of naïve pride in his voice.

Craig nodded.

'I did. And I'm inclined to agree with you that it was worth it if it has helped him to give a performance like the one he's putting over now.'

'Worth it?' Burton Malone smiled. 'After all you have been through it is very nice of you to say so. I do hope you'll forgive me for putting your secretary on the spot like that. Shocking for her, though I must say she looked cool and collected enough when she arrived. A very charming girl. Thank God it wasn't Claire.'

Craig grinned a trifle bleakly.

'My secretary is a very charming girl. But don't apologize. It's all in the day's work. I won't say I didn't offer up a mild prayer of thanks for spotting the chauffeur was a phoney when I did. It was only just a thought I had that he wasn't the same one I'd seen you with this morning when I noticed the car after dropping Miss Lamont at your house. I have a suspicious mind, so I checked up and when I had a good look at him over the match he offered me, I knew he was a fake. That sent me snooping and I found your real chauffeur tied up in the garage minus his uniform.'

'Poor fellow,' put in Malone. 'He seems to be suffering from shock more than anything.'

'That — and a bump as big as an egg on the back of his head where they slugged him. Anyway, all the rest of the story that some snatch-boys had read about your daughter going to the Albert Hall, stuck out like that phoney chauffeur's rainbow-corner tie.'

'Tie?'

'His uniform was too tight round the neck and he couldn't fasten it properly. When he leaned over and lit my cigarette it gaped and showed his own collar and eye-catching tie underneath. That's what started me thinking.'

'You're a wonder,' said Burton Malone.

Craig looked modest.

'Just a private dick,' he said blandly.

3

The Houseboat Shooting

Mist curled up from the river like silent ghosts. A distant tug's siren echoed eerily. Overhead the sky was black and starless.

Simone hung on to Craig's arm, which he didn't mind a bit, as they made their way along the towpath below Kew Bridge. They were looking for the riverside bungalow of Inspector Lumley. The Inspector was an old friend and had asked Craig to look him up; he thought he had a little job he could put his way.

A dark mass loomed up out of the river on their right and Craig muttered:

'This is the houseboat, anyway. Lumley's bungalow should be about fifty yards along.'

Simone suggested in her husky French accent:

'Perhaps there are more houseboats?'

'Shouldn't be,' Craig said. 'This is the

only one along this stretch of the river. Anyway, we'll soon check up. 'Shangri-la', the houseboat's named.' He produced his cigarette lighter. 'Bound to be the name-board about here — '

He broke off and Simone's grip on his arm tightened suddenly.

'What was that?' she asked.

He paused before saying, casually:

'Could be just a car backfiring somewhere. Or — could be a shot.'

'It seemed to come from the house-boat.'

'In which case,' he said, 'chances are it was someone cutting loose with a gun. They wouldn't be driving a car round their sitting room.'

Craig found a small gate, which admitted them onto a railed gangplank.

'Watch your step,' he told Simone as he led the way, and Simone followed close behind him. The river ran black beneath them, lapping against the sides of the houseboat.

Craig pressed the bell of the front door. It opened almost at once and a woman stood framed in the doorway. She was in evening dress, with gardenias in her blonde hair. Her eyes were round with apprehension.

'We were just passing,' Craig said pleasantly, 'and thought we heard a shot.'

'It's my husband,' she gasped. 'He — he's dead.'

'Who is it, Marion?' a voice called out behind her, and a man hurried forward. 'Who is it?' he asked again, his tone hitting a high note.

Craig said the speech he'd made to the woman over again. The man eyed him sharply, then patted the woman's arm.

'All right, Marion, I'll take care of this. The doctor's on his way.'

Edging himself into the narrow hall, Craig said:

'Maybe I can be of some help?'

'Who are you?'

Craig introduced himself, and the man said:

'In that case you couldn't have called at a more opportune moment. I'm afraid this will have to be a police job, anyway. Come in.'

Craig raised an eyebrow at him and

stepped inside, Simone following him.

'I shot him,' the other went on quietly, and Simone gave a little gasp. 'It was an accident of course,' the man continued. 'Thornton was showing me one of his revolvers, I didn't know it was loaded and it went off.'

'Where is he?' Craig said.

The woman answered him.

'In his room. Richard,' to the man, 'will you show him?'

Craig went along with the other, whose name was Winslow, to a small room. A middle-aged man lay collapsed in a deep chair.

Craig took a look at him and shook his head grimly. He glanced round at the walls covered with sporting prints and photographs, hung with swords and foils, plus various other sporting trophies. On the table lay several revolvers and a pair of old-fashioned pistols.

Craig glanced at Winslow.

'You say he was showing you one of these when it went off?'

Winslow nodded.

'Which was the gun?'

46

Winslow handed him a squat-looking revolver, which Craig broke. It held four rounds of ammunition.

'Were you alone with him when it happened?'

'Yes. Mrs. Thornton was in the bedroom. The others were in the sitting room.'

'Others?'

'Mr. and Mrs. Greenway. It was just a little party. We were going to play cards afterwards. Then, after dinner, Thornton — he was mad about his collection of guns — asked me to have a look at those two French pistols he'd just bought.'

Craig glanced at the two heavily ornamented pistols on the table. The other was continuing:

'After I'd looked at them, he handed me this other one, asking if I'd seen it the last time I was here. I'm afraid I don't know anything about guns — frankly I've always been nervous of them — and I took it from him without thinking. He never warned me it was loaded. I must have pulled the trigger. There was a terrific report and he fell down.'

Craig looked at the inert figure

slumped in the chair. He said to Winslow:

'The bullet hit him in the chest. You couldn't have done better if you meant to kill him.'

'That's an uncalled-for remark — !' the other exclaimed hotly.

Craig said, through a cloud of cigarette smoke:

'Take it easy. I'm not accusing anybody. You say,' he went on calmly, 'Mrs. Thornton was in her bedroom? Where is it? And maybe she would like to tell me what she did — '

'She rushed in — ' began the other, but Craig interrupted him.

'I'd like to hear it in her own words,' he said.

The other nodded and went out.

Craig took another look round the room and stared for a moment at the inert figure in the chair. Suddenly he noticed the watch was hanging awry from his waistcoat pocket. The watch-chain had snapped. Craig drew at his cigarette and then went into the bedroom.

Mrs. Thornton joined him almost immediately.

'You want to ask me some questions?' Her voice was low and unemotional,

He shot her a look. She'd got herself pretty well under control, he thought. He said:

'You were here when your husband was shot?'

'Yes,' she said. 'I — I rushed into the other room and saw him collapsing on the floor. Richard said something about it was an accident. The gun had gone off. He was horror-stricken. Then he pulled himself together and I helped him get my husband into the chair. Then I ran out to the others who were in the sitting room. They calmed me and, just as I was going back to the study, you arrived.'

Craig stared at her thoughtfully. She was trembling. At that moment, Simone came in with a drink.

'Drink this, Mrs. Thornton. It will do you good.'

The woman threw Simone a grateful smile and took the glass. As she did so, something glinting beside a table leg caught Craig's eye and he bent swiftly and picked it up He said, casually:

'Maybe I could have a word with your friends in the other room?'

Greenway was a tall, heavy-featured individual, his wife blue-eyed and fluffy. Both appeared overcome by the tragedy and corroborated Winslow's and the woman's story so far as they could.

'I was always scared of those revolvers,' Mrs. Greenway said. 'I felt there'd be an accident one of these days.'

'Nonsense,' protested her husband. 'Thornton always took the greatest care. It was young Winslow's fault, obviously — '

He stopped short with embarrassment as Winslow came in, followed by Mrs. Thornton.

'I've already admitted I was to blame for the ghastly business,' he said with bitterness. He glanced at Craig. 'Haven't I?'

For answer, Craig stepped forward and picked something from Winslow's lapel. It was an iron-grey hair.

There was a little silence. Nobody moved. Only the moan of a distant tug-siren cut into the stillness.

Craig nodded at Winslow and said nonchalantly:

'Supposing you cut the heroics and give me the facts? And — ' as the other started to speak, 'don't ask me what I mean. I just know you're trying to shield Mrs. Thornton — '

There was a sharp exclamation from the woman.

'What the devil are you getting at?' demanded Winslow.

Craig sighed. He said, patiently:

'You and she were in the bedroom. Thornton came in with his gun — maybe he was the jealous husband type. There was a struggle, during which his watch-chain snapped.' To Mrs. Thornton, who was staring at the watch-chain link, which glinted in his hand, he said: 'You got the gun from him and it went off. While you rushed in here, he turned again to Winslow and dragged the body into the chair. That's how you got Thornton's hair caught in your lapel — '

Winslow made a sudden movement and the squat-looking revolver appeared in his hand.

'All right, Mr. Clever,' he snapped. 'That'll do for now. Don't move, or this time I will shoot.' To the woman: 'Get out of here, quick as you can. I'll take care of him — or anybody else who tries to stop you.'

'Aren't you making a second mistake?' Craig queried.

'Second — ?'

Craig's smile was chilly. He said levelly:

'You said that gun killed Thornton, but not a round in it has been fired — that's how I knew you were lying when you said you'd shot him. Another gun did that job. And anyway,' he added, 'even if you fired it now, the cartridges happen to be blanks.'

Winslow's jaw sagged and he glanced at the revolver. Which was all Craig needed. Moving in like a flash he draped a punch on the other's jaw that stuck and dropped him like a log.

Afterwards, Simone said:

'Did you have to knock the poor young man out like that? After all, he couldn't have hurt you with those blank cartridges.'

Craig grinned at her.

'Blanks nothing. You were just hearing me talk myself out of a nasty corner. The gun held four rounds that would have riddled me like a sieve.'

4

The Girl in Dark Glasses

Bruce Kershaw was very much in love with Margot Delling. But the snag was the old one. He had no money.

'It's hopeless, Margot darling,' he said from where he sat facing her over the little table in the corner of the café where they met most mornings for coffee.

She was looking down at her plate.

'How much do you owe, Bruce?'

'Three thousand,' he answered bitterly. 'A nice round little sum, isn't it?'

'I suppose your aunt wouldn't — ?' she suggested tentatively.

'We've been over it so many times before.' He covered one of her hands with his. 'It's no good, Margot. At least, I'm no good. I wish to heavens I'd never heard of Arthur Hill or his gaming parties.'

She glanced at her watch.

'I shall have to go,' she told him.

'They'll be missing me at the shop.'

'I'll take you back.'

'Better not,' she smiled at him. 'It wouldn't do for them to see I'd been out with you. They might not approve of me slipping away from work to meet a man. But don't worry too much, darling. We'll think of something.'

He paid the bill and they said goodbye on the pavement.

'I'll give you a ring this evening,' he told her. 'And don't you go wearing yourself out at that shop.'

She gave him her promise with a smile that trembled a little and he watched her slim figure hurry along the street. No wonder he loved her, he thought: she was utterly wonderful. He sighed and turned to go in the opposite direction.

Margot Delling rounded the corner and hailed a taxi, and the address she gave the driver was not the name of the florist's where she worked.

A little later in an outer office on the first floor of an office block, she was saying:

'I'd like to see Mr. Craig.'

Simone looked up.

'Have you an appointment?'

The girl shook her head.

'I'm afraid not. My name is Margot Delling. I would be grateful if Mr. Craig would see me now — if he's not too busy.'

'I'll find out for you.'

Simone went through the frosted-glass door.

'A girl called Margot Delling wants to see you.'

'What's she like?'

'Young and very pretty — what you can see of her.'

Craig looked at her.

'What's the matter, is she wearing a yashmak?'

'She is wearing the most enormous pair of dark glasses I've ever seen.'

'Intrigue,' Craig grinned. 'Send her in at once.'

Simone smiled and a moment later 'Intrigue' was seating herself in the chair Craig offered her.

'It is really most awfully good of you, Mr. Craig,' she smiled apologetically. 'I ought to have made an appointment but

I have just left — someone — the man I'm going to marry — and I came here on the spur of the moment.'

'Heart trouble?' murmured Craig solicitously.

Her smile became bleak.

'Trouble,' she corrected him.

Craig waited patiently for her to start. She did so by touching the glasses she was wearing.

'By the way, I do hope you don't mind these. They are very disconcerting to people, I know, but I am suffering from eyestrain and the doctor has advised me to wear them for a few days.'

'It doesn't worry me. How about telling me your story?'

'His name is Bruce Kershaw,' she began. 'I — I'm crazy about him but he is terribly weak. He's — he's been gambling. I don't approve at all, and I don't know what to do. It's an awful mess.'

Craig raised an amused eyebrow. 'We all like a little flutter now and again, Miss Delling.'

'This isn't a little flutter,' she said earnestly. 'He has been going to gambling parties given by a man called Arthur Hill.'

Craig raised the other eyebrow.

'I know him. How much does this bloke of yours owe Hill?'

'Three thousand.'

'And I suppose he hasn't got a penny to bless himself with?'

She shook her head.

'He lives with a very rich aunt who holds the purse strings. She has jewellery worth a great deal, and — and Hill says that — that maybe, she doesn't hide it all away and she wouldn't miss some anyway. It is just left like that, Mr. Craig. Just those awful hints. Putting temptation in Bruce's way.'

Craig put in gently:

'But your boyfriend says, 'No, no, a thousand times, no', and Hill replies that if he doesn't pay up by such-and-such a date he'll rush round to Auntie demanding his dues.'

The girl looked up quickly.

'Yes, that's right. But how did you know?' There was surprise in her voice.

Craig grinned.

'A detective is not only trained to spot

the slip-up the criminal makes, he should even foresee the mistake the crook is going to make.'

She didn't smile back.

'Bruce has nothing,' she said miserably, 'and there is no one he can turn to for money.'

Craig looked at her quizzically.

'What do you expect me to do about it? I am neither a philanthropic institution nor much good at softening the hearts of hard-headed relatives.'

'I thought — if you would just see this man Hill and persuade him to leave Bruce alone. Maybe you could frighten him into it,' she added hopefully, then, as she caught the expression on his face: 'Couldn't you?'

Craig shook his head.

'With a sinister-looking gun?' he said ironically. 'Look, I'm sorry for all this mess. It's tough for you. But if I went to Hill, you know what he'd say, don't you? Simply that he is owed money and naturally, he would like to have it. But he'll deny with his last breath he ever suggested your boyfriend should pinch his aunt's sparklers to pay him back. Or that he used any threats at all. He'd call it a so-and-so lie — and I can't say I'd blame him.'

'Then you don't think you can do anything?'

'I'm afraid not. My tip is for Kershaw to go to his aunt and spill the bag of beans.'

'You don't know Aunt Flora. If she knew he had lost all that gambling, she would throw him out — and we would be further from marrying than ever. Not that she'd care. She doesn't approve of me.'

'She must have remarkably bad judgement,' murmured Craig.

'I work in a florist's,' Margot Delling explained. 'I'm not supposed to be good enough for her precious nephew.'

'Ridiculous,' Craig sympathized. He added, 'Not to say old-fashioned.'

She turned her face towards the window.

'Yes, isn't it? Are you sure there is no way to stop this man carrying out his threat?'

'If I dream up anything,' Craig assured

her, 'I'll let you know. But don't count on it.'

'Well, anyway, thank you for your time.' She smiled uncertainly and stood up. 'Goodbye.'

When she had gone he went into the other office.

'I'm on my way out,' he informed Simone. 'Hold any customers with large bank balances.'

She smiled.

'I'll do just that little thing,' she promised him.

'I'm afraid,' Craig said, 'that you are picking up a lot of tough talk from me. I'm doing you no good.'

'You'd be surprised,' she said. But he was gone, en route to a large block of flats overlooking Oxford Street, and one flat in particular.

When he arrived he kept his finger on the bell-push until the door was finally opened to him by a blonde who looked as if she had seen better days.

'Mr. Hill?'

She looked at him up and down with tired but shrewd eyes.

'Come in,' she invited, her jaws working with a kind of rhythmic precision on a mutilated piece of chewing gum.

Arthur Hill put down the cup of black coffee he had been drinking and gazed at his visitor wonderingly.

'Well, I ain't seen you for a hell of a time,' he announced with obvious delight. 'What's the trouble? I ain't in any — I hope?' he added anxiously.

'Not this time,' said Craig, smiling. He always enjoyed Arthur Hill's child-like humour. 'Not yet.'

'Whadya mean, not yet? I'm a pretty careful boy these days. Coffee?'

'No thanks.'

Craig sat on the edge of the divan bed.

Arthur Hill looked across at the blonde standing with a kind of bovine docility in the doorway. 'Get to hell outa here,' he yelled. 'I'll be seeing you. Usual place.'

The woman stared at him placidly, nodding once or twice, flashed Craig a toothy smile and a moment later the front door slammed.

'Now,' Hill said comfortably, 'what's it you got on your mind?'

'Up to a point — you.'

Craig told him Margot Delling's story in a few clipped sentences and watched Hill's jaw sag with some sort of satisfaction.

'Well I'll be — ! Aw, Craig, you know me. I'll say you know me. Maybe we had a coupla little arguments way back — that's how these things go. But did you ever know me to touch hot jools — I ask you?'

'Not that I'm aware of,' Craig said mildly. 'Up to date.'

'Up to date. C'mon, C'mon. You know my racket like I do and I ain't ever dealt in that kind of a mug's game. I admit this darned kid owes me three thousand, but his girl's crazy yarn of me wanting him to knock off his aunt's bric-a-brac is wacky. Hell, what does she think I am — ?'

The indignation in his tone made Craig grin again.

'I have no idea,' he said.

On the full tide of his wrath, Arthur Hill swept on.

'*I knows* a coupla dopes who trade in that sort of stuff,' he admitted. 'But that don't make me one of 'em.'

'Who are they?' asked Craig idly. 'The information could be helpful.'

The information was helpful.

So helpful it induced Craig to put in a phone call to Scotland Yard almost directly after he had left Arthur Hill's flat. Then he went back to see if Simone was free for lunch. She was.

★   ★   ★

Three days later, the slim figure of a girl came slipping quietly out of a house in Park Gardens, off Berkeley Square, into a very early morning mist.

She had left a downstairs window open and now she carried a small bundle under her loose tweed coat. She reached the street and glanced rapidly up and down. It was deserted. The figure ducked into a car that was parked a little way along the kerb.

She spoke no word and the driver, who had been as silent as she on the drive to a certain block of flats, broke the spell as he pulled up.

'Everything okay?'

'Okay,' she told him tersely, alighting on the pavement. 'You'd better get going.'

He nodded and as she entered the block the car slid off down the street.

Ten minutes later the girl was putting her bundle down on the table of the flat's living room for the inspection of an urbane dark gentleman wearing a silk dressing gown and smoking a Turkish cigarette in an amber holder.

'You got everything worth having?'

Her lip curled.

'It was too easy.'

She undid the bundle and spilt the jewels out on to the table and her companion's eyes glittered.

'At a quick guess,' he hazarded softly, 'I'll say they're worth having. And it is going to be too easy from now on.'

'Thanks to me,' the girl retorted. 'I keep telling you, you're lucky to have me around.'

'Which is why he will accompany you when you leave,' said a deep voice from behind them. 'Pardon the intrusion,' it went on with heavy humour as the pair spun round to face a burly figure filling the doorway.

'I popped in because it's getting a bit nippy waiting outside the bathroom window — oh, no, you don't.' The man with the amber cigarette-holder had tried with a clumsy movement to cover up the jewels. 'No need to get all excited. No need at all. I've got a couple of friends with me.'

The man and the girl stared dumbly at the two plainclothes men looming behind Inspector Hooper. Chattily the Inspector remarked:

'Nice little haul you've got there, Gibson. Miss Kershaw would have been upset missing them.' Then as suddenly the banter left his voice. 'All right,' he snapped, 'Let's be moving.'

The girl, the man and the police, with Inspector Hooper plus the jewellery, moved.

★ ★ ★

A little later that same morning, when the grey dawn mists had been dispersed for quite a few hours, Craig was having his breakfast and glancing through his morning paper. He happened to catch the Stop Press with a sleepy eye.

'EARLY MORNING JEWEL ROBBERY'

'MAN AND GIRL DETAINED'

'In the early hours of this morning Flora Kershaw was robbed of jewellery at home in Park Gardens, W. 1. Police detained Tack Gibson, West End florist, and his wife in connection with robbery.'

A smile flitted across his lips but his reverie was broken by the ring of the telephone.

'Hallo?'

It was Simone.

'I shall be late,' Craig said quickly, anticipating her.

'I guessed that.' Her laugh came down the wire to him. 'I just rang to see if you were coming in at all this morning.'

'Any clients?'

'A Mr. Bruce Kershaw has been waiting the best part of an hour.'

Craig said:

'I'll be there.'

When he arrived in the office he found Simone and Bruce Kershaw apparently on chatty terms.

Craig interrupted the conversation.

'Come in,' he said to Kershaw.

The boy was still wearing a slightly stunned expression.

'I got most of the story from the police,' he said, taking one of Craig's cigarettes. 'I still can't believe it. They sent me to you.'

'It will be a bit hard for you to grasp. It was a nice little scheme on the part of the Gibson girl, alias Delling, and her husband to frame you or Arthur Hill, or both, with the jewel robbery.'

Kershaw groaned.

'She — and I thought — and she was married all the time.' His young voice took on a bitterness. 'Just digging information out of me about where Aunt's jewellery was kept.'

Craig said quietly:

'You're not the first she's worked on. If that's any comfort, which I don't suppose it is.'

'It's been a hell of a shock,' admitted the other ruefully. 'But I suppose I'm lucky to have come out of it as well as I have. Aunt Flora would have lost all that priceless stuff and I would have been suspected of stealing it, into the bargain. I'm very grateful to you, Mr. Craig, for all you've done.'

'I didn't do a thing,' said Craig honestly. 'Except tip off Scotland Yard. The Gibsons are old friends of theirs though I never met them before.'

'All the same, when — when Margot came to you with that story you saw through it. There are two things I don't understand.'

'What?'

'Why she came to you in the first place?'

'Because I didn't know her and she wanted your financial situation to be well and truly spread to the police.'

'Yes, of course. I was silly not to think of that myself,' said Bruce Kershaw

69

slowly. 'What about the other? How did you spot her story was crooked at the start?'

Craig grinned.

'As I seem to remember mentioning to her, a detective — that is, a good detective, like me,' he grinned modestly, 'should not only spot the slip the crook makes, he should also foresee the mistake he is going to make. She had already tripped herself up when she tried to kid me Arthur Hill was a fence. As you know, he does very nicely, thank you, out of his gaming parties.'

Bruce Kershaw grimaced.

'I know. Aunt Flora gave me the works.'

Craig continued:

'Like all of his kind Arthur Hill sticks strictly to his line of business and would never get tangled up with receiving stolen goods. Then I waited for the slip-up I foresaw she would make. She obliged.'

'How?'

Craig tapped some ash off his cigarette.

'It was slight,' he admitted, 'only just enough to raise my suspicions even more and send me on a check-up errand to my old friend Arthur Hill. She elaborated her fairy-story with a bit about your aunt thinking she wasn't good enough for you because she worked in a florist's — '

'A lie too.'

'I thought it was a bit too old-fashioned to be true, at the time,' he grinned. 'I even told her so. Arthur Hill supplied the rest. He told me about a Mr. and Mrs. Gibson, who ran a flower shop with a nifty sideline in hot sparklers. He also reminded me how, when they were pinched before, a lot of fuss was made by the newspaper boys about her oddly innocent look. Quite a talker, our Arthur.'

'By her 'innocent look' I suppose you mean her eyes?'

Craig nodded.

'One brown and the other blue. Maybe she was self-conscious about them — that's why she hid them behind a large pair of dark glasses.'

5

The Snap Answer

Craig had just finished shaving when they telephoned to say that the girl had been found. He finished dressing and went unhurriedly down to Scotland Yard. There was no need for haste; he could take it easy now. The casebook, so far as he and poor Lucy were concerned, was closed.

Yesterday afternoon he had looked in at the Arkwrights' café in Soho for some cigarettes and, instead of his usual warm welcome from old Pa and Ma Arkwright, had found them distraught.

'What's on your mind, Pa?'

Craig leaned one elbow on the counter and offered the old man a cigarette out of the new packet.

'It's Lucy.'

Pa's red face was shining and anxious above his white overalls. He jerked his head towards the back room. 'Ma's in there. Can't do anything with 'er she's that worried.'

'What's happened to Lucy?'

'She's gorn, Mr. Craig. Disappeared, and there's no one to know where she's got to.'

Craig raised an eyebrow.

'You mean she's run away?'

It seemed unlike Lucy Arkwright to him, and Pa was shaking his head.

'We don't know. But it don't hardly seem likely. She was always a good daughter to us, and we was an 'appy family, as you might say. Never a misunderstanding nor cross word. Lucy used to tell us things that were on 'er mind and — well, I just don't know what to think!'

Pa Arkwright wiped his big hand across his eyes and shuffled about unnecessarily with the day's menu card stuck up on the counter.

After a while Craig said:

'When did she disappear?'

'Last night. She was going out for a walk with someone, she said. We never thought to ask where, or 'oo she was

73

meeting. Lucy was a sensible girl, and Ma and me never 'ad thought it right to probe into 'er affairs. Only, she didn't come back, Mr. Craig. We 'aven't seen 'er since.'

'Have you informed the police?'

Pa nodded wretchedly.

'We done that, first thing this morning when she didn't turn up. Poor Ma, in there, is fair off 'er 'ead with the worry of it.'

Craig laid a hand on the old man's shoulder.

'All right, Pa. Try not to worry. I'll see what I can do to find Lucy for you.'

Old Pa Arkwright's eyes filled with tears again as he tried to smile.

'Will you, Mr. Craig? It would be good of you — ' He broke off, distressed. 'I — I that is, I can't afford — '

'Forget it,' Craig told him easily. 'We're old friends.'

After that he had checked round all Lucy's haunts he knew about. He checked up on her known friends — and drew blanks. He had been going to go round to the Arkwrights' in search of more information that morning. Instead, he thought bitterly, here he was, on his way to Scotland Yard.

Lucy Arkwright had been found — dead.

He went straight up to Inspector Holt's office. He hadn't seen the Inspector since the Frensham case.

'How are you?'

He grabbed the hard chair in front of the big desk.

'Fine.'

Inspector Holt and his Sergeant were busying themselves over photographs and reports and the office was hazy from the Inspector's blackened pipe. He threw down a paper and looked up at Craig. 'Sorry, we're not very conversational this morning,' he apologized. 'It's rather tough.'

'Nothing to go on?'

Craig lit a cigarette.

'Not much. The body was found in Regent's Park behind a clump of bushes, and the time of death, as near as we can estimate, was between ten p.m. and midnight night before last.'

The Sergeant said, 'A park-keeper found the body. Bit of a shock for him.'

'Nothing like the shock it is going to be for her father and mother,' Craig said. 'Have they been told yet?'

'Yes,' replied Holt heavily.

'Tell me more,' invited Craig.

'Well, it looks like a manslaughter job to us. The doctor thinks she died from the effects of a violent blow in the face. Apparently her heart wasn't all it should be. Whoever did the hitting probably panicked when he realized she was dead and beat it.'

'*He?*'

Holt ruffled through some papers on the desk and said irritably to the Sergeant:

'Where the hell's that snapshot found in her handbag?'

The Sergeant picked up an ashtray and fished beneath it.

'Here, sir.'

'Mm'mm . . . Make anything of it, Craig?'

Craig took the photo, remarking idly:

'So you *have* got something.'

'The only thing. I hate these find-the-body hit-and-run cases. There is never anything to get your teeth into.'

Craig slanted his cigarette ceilingwards and squinted at the picture through half-closed eyes.

'It's Lucy all right. And the chap's face is familiar too.'

He turned the picture over and read, 'Ron and me at Wembley'. He looked up as he felt Holt's eyes upon him, and met the scrutiny blandly.

'What do you mean — his face is familiar? If you have any ideas on the subject — '

Craig shrugged.

'I haven't. Only I've seen him around somewhere.'

He regarded the snapshot again thoughtfully.

'It was taken at Wembley, all right, sir,' the Sergeant volunteered over his shoulder. 'That's the Stadium in the distance. Nice clear snap too,' he added appreciatively. 'You can see the number of the bus coming down the road. Eighty-one.'

'It's not the bus we're interested in, Sergeant,' snapped Holt.

'No, sir.'

Craig was racking his brains trying to connect up that profile.

'It was taken recently,' the Inspector offered. 'The print is clear and fresh.'

Craig threw the snap back on to the desk.

'No good,' he said. 'At the moment, anyway.'

'Wish you could remember.'

'I will,' promised Craig. 'I'll go and pay a visit on Ma and Pa Arkwright, they'll be feeling pretty low but I might get something to help us.'

'You might,' Holt replied without much conviction.

Ma Arkwright was upstairs in her room with her eldest son and a couple of her sisters who were attempting to comfort her when Craig arrived in Soho.

'Ma's bad,' Pa said brokenly. 'She collapsed when — when the police told us wot 'appened.'

Craig said:

'But we have got to find out what happened to Lucy.' As Pa Arkwright showed signs of breaking up himself at the mention of his daughter's name, he said quickly, 'Will you try and help?'

'I'll try,' the old man said again, wiping his bald head with a large silk handkerchief.

'To start with, then, who was Lucy's latest boyfriend?'

Pa looked bewildered.

'There were so many, Mr. Craig. She wasn't never serious about no one.'

Craig knew that. There had always been plenty hanging round Lucy with her dark provocative eyes and warm smile.

'But that wouldn't rule out anyone being serious about her?'

'No. I knowed there was some as wanted to marry 'er. But Lucy just used to laugh and say she couldn't leave 'er 'ome for any of 'em. Proper 'ome bird, our Lucy was.'

'I know, Pa, I know. But can't you just remember the last one who wanted to know what size she took in wedding rings?'

'There was that Tony Delmonte 'oo works at that pintable place in Oxford Street. But Lucy didn't go out with 'im above a few times. She didn't like 'im no more nor we did. Too flashy for 'er.'

'Delmonte?'

Craig was frowning. 'Flashy' was one way of describing that character. He'd had a few encounters with Delmonte himself in the past, and he decided to do a little checking up in that quarter. He asked:

'Anyone else?'

'Not that we knowed of, Mr. Craig — Oh! There was some young boxer, I think, but we never met 'im.'

Craig stood up.

'Thanks, Pa. I'll work around those two. You've given me something to go on anyway.'

Out in the street he grabbed a taxi for Scotland Yard once more.

Some young boxer . . . He was back in a ringside seat at the Crescent Club. At his eye-level the two boys were toe to toe beneath the bluish glare of the arcs. The one in the green satin shorts being that promising light-weight, Ronnie 'Kid' Glover, who carried a punch in his right paw that would pole-axe a bull — *and whose profile was the dead spit of the one in the photo on Holt's desk.*

Early that evening they picked up the Kid and brought him into Inspector Holt's office. Craig was there as part of the welcoming committee.

'What do you know of Lucy Arkwright?' the Inspector asked without preamble.

'Never heard of her,' the Kid said promptly.

The Inspector sighed.

'When did you last see her?'

The Kid stuck to his guns.

'I tell you I never heard of her,' he said doggedly. 'Was she blonde or brunette? I only go for the blondes,' he added grinning.

'What were your movements night before last?'

The Kid appeared to be lost in thought. 'Night before last. That was the night I did nothing much.'

'You did nothing much,' the Inspector said sarcastically. '*What did you do?*'

'I'm telling you aren't I?' the Kid said aggressively. 'I had a work-out at the gym in Edgware Road, far as I remember, then I had a bite in a milk-bar and strolled

81

along trying to make up my mind what I *would* do for the evening.'

'And when you made up your mind?' the Inspector asked and he sounded as if he was ready to disbelieve whatever story the Kid put forward.

'I strolled on to Marble Arch.'

'By yourself, naturally.'

'As it happens, I was. I went along Oxford Street looked in at one or two amusement arcades.'

Craig said lazily from his corner:

'The one where Tony Delmonte works?'

'Who the hell's Tony Delmonte? If you would all stop interrupting I'd be able to tell you what I did do. I took a bus to Piccadilly, walked on down the Strand where I had a glass of beer, hung about a bit and came roughly the same way home.'

'You didn't go to the cinema, I suppose?' asked the inspector, his voice heavily sarcastic.

'No,' was all the Kid answered. 'I didn't feel like a movie. I just made my way home. Got back about eleven and went straight to bed.'

The Inspector nodded humourlessly.

'You must have felt quite tired after all that walking about.' There was a pause, while the Inspector, timing it like an actor delivering a dramatic line, said, 'And you still say you never met Lucy Arkwright in your life?'

And he shoved the snapshot under the Kid's nose.

'Well, I'll be — '

The Kid broke off, gazing at the picture.

'Yes?' Inspector Holt asked, his eyes snapping with triumph.

The Kid laughed.

' 'Course, I don't know her,' he said easily. 'I keep telling you, don't I? That's not me. Look at his left ear and look at mine. I always was wide open to a straight right,' he added ruefully.

The Inspector glanced at him. Then he snatched back the photograph. Craig sauntered round the desk.

He looked at the Kid and then at the snapshot. Whereas the Kid's left ear had been battered into the cauliflower shape typical of the pugilist, the man in the photograph was unmarked. The Kid was grinning jauntily.

'See what I mean? Must have a double, mustn't I?'

'You certainly must,' returned the Inspector bitterly. He slanted a baffled glare up at Craig.

Craig smiled sweetly back at him.

'Don't take it too hard, Inspector.'

Inspector Holt nodded to the Sergeant. 'All right,' he said wearily.

As the door closed behind the Kid, Craig remarked:

'Better be getting along too.'

'Start looking for a double of the Kid then,' Inspector Holt called after him.

'Not a bad idea, at that.'

Craig caught up with the Kid in the street. In the most friendly fashion he took his arm.

'Let's get a cup of coffee apiece.'

'Why?'

Craig steered him adroitly into a little café. As they found a corner table and parked themselves, the Kid stared at him uneasily.

'What's on your mind?'

'This.'

Craig flipped the photograph over the table.

The Kid sneered:

'What the devil you driving at? I told that flatfoot in there it wasn't me. And I proved it too, didn't I?'

Craig grinned at him.

'Inspector Holt has had a busy day otherwise he would have seen what I saw.'

The Kid gave him an ugly look.

'Well, come on,' he challenged. 'What did you see?'

'A bus,' Craig said cryptically.

'A — a bus?'

'That's the idea. You see, Kid, the eighty-one bus doesn't run through Wembley, it's the eighteen that does that — the number on the negative when it's printed the right side up. You forgot to mention to Inspector Holt the snap had been printed the wrong way round, and what he took for your left ear, was really your right — '

As the Kid let loose the punch that had won him his last twenty-seven bouts, and with which in a jealous rage he had killed Lucy Arkwright, Craig's hands grabbed the table. Next moment the Kid was lying flat on his back with the table and two cups of steaming coffee on top of him.

'Kid,' Craig looked down at him sadly, 'you could have been a great boxer if only you had learned to keep your temper.'

6

The Invalid Chess Player

There was a cold draught filtering through the half-open door of the library as Mrs. Wycombe stared over her husband's head at Dr. Sutton.

'Well?'

The doctor straightened up, but his eyes still rested on the immobile fragile form of Leonard Wycombe in his invalid chair by the window.

'I think,' he said slowly, 'you had better telephone the police.'

As Mrs. Wycombe turned without answering he added sharply:

'Mind that hypodermic on the floor.'

She walked to the telephone and picked up the receiver.

Dr. Sutton sighed and looked out of the window into the garden where the shadows were already lengthening.

'It's cold in here,' he remarked.

The woman went on dialling but said in a flat voice:

'It's the front door. It's probably open again. Hallo? This is Mrs. Wycombe.'

Dr. Sutton shifted his gaze from the window to her.

He would never understand her. She was as cool and unruffled as if nothing had happened. Or perhaps it was merely that she was still dazed and it made her talk into the phone in that curiously monotonous voice. Dr. Sutton looked down at his late patient as Mrs. Wycombe's voice came to him across the room.

'Suicide. Yes. I'd appreciate it if you would.'

She rang off.

'They are coming over immediately,' she said.

Dr. Sutton nodded and taking off his pince-nez began to wipe them nervously. If she would only break down a bit. It must be a strain for her. And yet, that was the very quality he had always admired in her, her complete disregard for the conventional, her control of herself at all times.

He supposed she had learned in a tough school with a husband years older than herself and an invalid at that. And she was a lovely woman. At that moment she turned her blonde head towards him and smiled a little, although when she spoke the monotone of her voice was the same.

'I think I'll go and close the front door. You're right about it being cold.'

She walked out into the hall. The next minute she snapped out of her passive manner.

A man had pushed the front door wider and was about to come in. She hurried forward.

'Are you the police? You've been quick enough. I'm Mrs. Wycombe.'

He raised an eyebrow at his unexpected welcome.

'No,' he responded, running his eye appraisingly over her, 'I am not the police. Sorry to disappoint you.'

She spoke quickly and breathlessly as the events of the evening at last seemed to crowd in on her. 'Then who are you and what do you want? This is rather an awkward moment. I'm afraid — my husband — '

'Is expecting me,' put in the man easily. 'The name is Craig. Private dick. Mr. Wycombe telephoned me to come over and see him. Seems he was scared about something.'

'Scared?' She stared at him. Then: 'Well, I'm afraid you've arrived too late. He is dead.'

'Murder?' Craig took out his cigarette case.

'Murder. What made you say that?'

'Just a trend of thought. Maybe he was scared of his own shadow.'

'My husband committed suicide,' she told him firmly, and moved over to the front door, closing it with a decisive slam. She nodded towards it. 'The catch has gone,' she explained. 'I must have it seen to.'

'Since I'm here and since, from what you say, the police are presumably on their way, I'd like to take a look at him.'

She supposed it would be all right, she said, and inclined her head towards the room she had just left.

'He's in there. I got back twenty minutes ago and found him. I telephoned Dr. Sutton at once. He is with him now, though of course, I knew my husband was dead and there was nothing that could be done. But Dr. Sutton told me to ring the police.'

'It must have been a shock for you.'

Craig followed her into the library.

As they entered the room, Dr. Sutton turned.

'You the police?'

Craig shook his head. Mrs. Wycombe answered the doctor:

'This is Mr. Craig, Dr. Sutton. He is a private detective. My husband apparently phoned him just before this happened. I can't imagine why. His mind — '

She left the sentence unfinished with a shrug of her shoulders. Craig was wondering what feelings she'd had for her husband.

'His mind must have been temporarily unbalanced,' said Dr. Sutton with professional matter-of-factness.

'What was the matter with him, Doctor?'

The other replaced his pince-nez.

'He was suffering from an acute rheumatic complaint which left him a cripple. He was frequently very depressed.'

'From which you deduct that this was suicide?'

'What else?' Dr. Sutton looked slightly shaken. 'It all points to suicide, don't you agree?'

Craig drew at his cigarette.

'Could be you're right,' he answered off-handedly. His eye alighted on the hypodermic lying on the floor. 'What did he inject himself with?'

'A shot of cyanide in the forearm. Scheele's Acid, to be exact.'

'Pretty fast working stuff?'

'Absolutely instantaneous.'

Craig whistled soundlessly and observed:

'Quite an original turn of mind. Most of 'em use a gun or a gas oven.'

The doctor nodded his agreement and offered his theory.

'Mr. Wycombe was being treated with injections. No doubt that is what gave him the idea.'

'No doubt.'

On the mantelpiece a large ornate clock of Chinese design ticked loudly. Craig's eyes flicked over his surroundings. A barn of a room, subtly and yet luxuriously furnished. It bore out Wycombe's insinuation that money was no object when he had talked to Craig and told him he was in danger of his life. A slight movement caught Craig's eye.

Dr. Sutton had bent down and picked up the hypodermic from the floor in an absent-minded fashion and was pushing in the projecting piston in order to fit it into its case which lay on a nearby table.

'You should have left that as you found it,' Craig reprimanded him gently. 'Police have a peculiar habit of preferring everything left untouched, you know. They are rather fussy about it.'

The doctor dropped the instrument at once and blinked nervously.

'I — I am terribly sorry,' he stammered. 'I'm afraid I wasn't thinking. I don't remember ever having had any dealings with the police like this.'

'No,' agreed Craig softly. 'I don't suppose you have.'

He sauntered nearer to the window and stood looking out on to the rapidly darkening garden. The sound of the traffic in the Finchley Road came in a droning hum to his ears. He glanced at his watch. He had been in the house about ten minutes.

He turned restlessly to a chessboard set out on the table. Picking up a piece which was lying beside the board, he twisted it idly between his thumb and forefinger. Then replacing it, he said:

'So Wycombe was a chess player?'

Mrs. Wycombe answered him.

'Yes. My husband was an enthusiast. I don't understand the game.'

'You mean he played by himself?' Craig queried.

'He played by telephone with a friend in Wimbledon. He was terribly touchy about anyone moving that board.'

Craig, smiling, left the board to itself and changed the subject.

'And you say when you came back you found your husband dead.'

She went over to the window and pulled the curtains before she answered him.

'I have already told you and the police will ask all the same questions.'

Her tone implied she was wondering what right Craig had to crash in anyway, but it merely had the effect of sending his eyebrow up.

'So you phoned for Doctor Sutton at once?'

'Of course.'

Craig's smile broadened and again he glanced at his watch.

'The police should be here any minute,' he said, half to himself, half to the company. 'Mr. Wycombe was alive half an hour before I arrived, because I spoke to him myself. It's hardly likely it was someone impersonating him. They wouldn't want me poking my nose into this business. What I want to know is, which one of you killed him?'

He spoke so quietly and conversationally that the stabbing reality of the words produced a delayed shock. Then his voice cut right through to the reeling senses of the man and the woman. Craig had brought back his gaze from the contemplation of a picture and fixed it on Sutton. 'My guess is that it was you,' he announced chattily. 'What's the matter, Mrs. Wycombe?'

The blonde had recoiled against the chess table, scattering the pieces onto the floor.

'Better be careful of that board,' Craig reminded her. 'But take it easy while I tell you just what happened — or rather, what didn't happen. If Wycombe injected himself with that cyanide, the way Dr. Sutton said he did, the piston of the hypodermic would have been pushed in — he wouldn't have had time to pull it out, even if he had wanted to, before he was dead. In the words of Dr. Sutton, death was instantaneous.'

He glanced at Dr. Sutton whose face had gone a slate grey and who seemed incapable of speech.

'That's why, dear Doctor,' Craig went on silkily, 'arriving at the same conclusion, only a little late, you shoved the piston back on my somewhat unexpected arrival. Now, perhaps if you wouldn't mind giving me the real facts.'

'You fool, Charles,' the woman flashed at the other, her eyes blazing.

Craig smiled.

'Charles?' he murmured. 'So that's the way the wind blows, is it?'

She choked.

'Do something, can't you.'

Sutton turned desperately to Craig.

'Listen,' he gabbled hoarsely, 'you've got to listen to me. She — she wasn't happy tied to that old man, a cripple. How could she be, a young and beautiful woman? It was a happy release for him — yes, that was what it was, a happy release.'

'I suppose you wouldn't have been influenced at all by the money she would have, would you?'

'Money?' Dr. Sutton's voice rose wildly. 'Money? Is that what you want? I swear I'll pay you anything — anything. Only keep quiet about this.'

Craig looked at him, drew deliberately at his cigarette and let the smoke curl slowly to the ceiling.

'Listen, Craig, you've got to listen. How much do you want, I'll pay you anything, only tell me quickly. We've got to be quick, the police will be here any minute — how much?'

Craig eyed him steadily.

'Dear me,' he drawled. 'You do judge others by your own standards, don't you?'

The other wasn't listening.

'Tell me — quickly — '

'Charles!'

It was the woman's voice that cut through the man's babbling. She was facing the door and staring transfixed at something.

'A little bird tells me,' Craig said without turning round, 'that the police have arrived.'

He teetered slowly on his heels and viewed the plainclothes men framed in the doorway without surprise

'I'm so glad,' he said. 'This conversation was beginning to bore me. I wouldn't have you go on talking except I knew the cops were on their way. It seemed a pity to waste them — but for them to walk right into the house without even ringing the bell — ' He turned to Mrs. Wycombe.

'You really must get that latch fixed.' He broke off. Then: 'Though, come to think of it, you won't be needing it now, will you?'

7

The Blonde and the Balcony

Craig had been occupied in St. John's Wood putting the finishing touches to a little case of unexpected murder, when he had gone out with nothing more in his head than to listen to the whims of an invalid old man.

At the end of it he felt suddenly in need of a few bright lights in the company of a brunette, which was good enough reason for him to step into a phone box and put through a call to his own office.

'I'd love to,' replied Simone promptly. 'Had a successful afternoon?'

'That and more. And you?'

'Dull,' said Simone.

He laughed.

'Meet me at the Cosmopolitan in half an hour,' he told her and rang off.

He hailed a taxi and arrived under the time he had estimated. It was therefore no surprise to him when he walked into the vestibule of the hotel and did not see Simone.

He paused before entering the bar to light a cigarette, and it was then he saw the blonde.

She was leaning over the desk talking earnestly to the clerk, and she was tall, slender, assured and a pleasure to gaze upon. Since Craig had nothing better to do at that particular moment, he took time off to light his cigarette in a leisurely way and feast his eyes.

During this manoeuvre the object of his fascination turned slightly away from the desk and began to drum two scarlet fingernails on the polished surface while the clerk picked up the house telephone.

From this new angle Craig had a better view. A much better view. She was more than a pleasure, she was literally beautiful. Her eyes, from that distance anyway, were a smoky blue, like a Siamese cat's, only this cat had long silky black lashes to frame her eyes. Her face was heart-shaped with a creamy complexion and a wide red mouth that looked — while searching in his mind for a suitable adjective the mouth in question curved up into a ghost of a smile, and then she turned back to the clerk. Those smoky eyes had certainly seen him and the smile, though so slight as to be almost an illusion, had certainly been a smile.

Craig drew nearer as the clerk replaced the receiver.

'I'm sorry, madam, but I can't get any reply from room twenty.'

Craig halted. He could hear the conversation and he wanted to know what sort of voice a girl with a face and figure like hers would own.

Anyway, he was of a naturally curious disposition.

'But it's too silly.'

The voice was every bit as exciting as he had thought it would be. It held the trace of an American accent, which was entrancing and added to its charm.

'I'm sorry,' the clerk said. 'Perhaps Mrs. Harrington is out?'

'I know she's not out. Her key is not here, is it?'

The clerk searched and said that it was not.

'Well, then.'

She gave a ripple of laughter; Craig thought it was more from nervousness than humour. She didn't look as if she could be the nervous type.

'See here,' she was saying. 'I have a room next my aunt's but I couldn't get any reply when I knocked this morning; nor at lunch time. In fact, she's just not answering.'

The clerk shook his head unhelpfully.

'Perhaps Mrs. Harrington does not wish to be disturbed.'

The girl tapped an impatient finger.

'It begins to look that way, doesn't it? It's just exactly what the room-maid told me this morning — but it's evening now and I'm getting kind of worried.'

The clerk looked sympathetic but could apparently offer no more suggestions and the blonde picked up a flat leather handbag and swung off in the direction of the American bar.

She was sitting on a high stool opposite the door with a rye-and-dry and swinging a nylon-clad leg. It was a very nice leg. Thoughtfully, Craig sauntered over to the stool next door to hers and parked himself.

'Make it a double,' he nodded to the barman.

The girl beside him was slipping a slender silver cigarette case, adorned with the initials 'M.M.', out of her handbag. She selected a cigarette. Craig took a chance and flipped his lighter into action.

'Light?'

She smiled at him and for the second time her eyes met his. He thought they were now a smoky green. Obviously she recognized him but she only murmured:

'Thanks.'

Then she turned away and swallowed her drink as if her life depended upon getting it down as fast as she could. She ordered another. Craig, watching, saw the way her hand shook as she pushed her empty glass away from her.

'Worried about something?' he asked with interest.

Slowly she turned towards him again, but this time her lovely eyebrows were arched in surprise.

'I beg your pardon?'

Blow hot, blow cold, thought Craig. She knew the ropes all right. He repeated his question and this time it was he that turned on the charm. This time she responded.

'As a matter of fact — yes.'

His smile widened to a grin.

'But you don't see what business it is of mine?'

She flashed him a look that was half angry, half amused, but Craig's grin won the day. Amusement was more apparent.

'I don't see how you knew,' she corrected him.

He looked at her quizzically.

'All part of the job,' he told her.

'What job?'

Craig didn't see why he should enlighten her. 'The job of the moment. I overheard your conversation with the clerk. Maybe your aunt has overslept.'

One side of her mouth curved upwards.

'All day?' she chided.

'Why not? A very nice occupation too.'

She took a deep drag at her cigarette and changed the subject rather hurriedly, he thought.

'I haven't seen her in two years.'

'A long time.'

She nodded agreement.

'I arrived late last night. I considered I was lucky to get a room at all, and extra lucky getting one right next door to my aunt.'

'You've only just arrived in London?'

'I've been in the States,' she said shortly, then: 'My aunt had gone to bed last night when I finally got here and I didn't like to disturb her. So far, she hasn't put in any sort of an appearance at all, and I'm getting a bit scary about the whole thing.'

Craig thought how beautiful she looked when she was scary.

'Does she know you're here?'

'No.' There was a distinct tremor in her voice. 'I'm afraid we never hit it off very well. And then, of course, when I married an American, it was the last straw for poor Auntie.' She laughed softly. 'She took an extremely poor view of the entire setup and swore I'd be back and asking for help.' She ended up wryly, 'She was right.'

'Too bad.'

She said briskly:

'Pete — my husband — just wasn't all he cooked himself up to be, that's all. It's the old, old story, I'm afraid, without any original angles at all. So here I am, back again.'

'And no money.'

'You're damned right. However,' she shrugged her shoulders slightly, 'Auntie is very well off. Does that sound hard and unpleasant — ?'

'On the contrary,' Craig told her firmly.

She smiled at him.

'I am just a little disillusioned,' she admitted. 'But I'd pay her back, honestly, just as soon as I can get a job. It — it would only be to tide me over settling down. Of course, she'll be really furious when she sees me, but she'd never let one of the family be absolutely on the rocks without forking out.'

'I'm sure she wouldn't,' Craig nodded pleasantly. 'How about another drink?'

'I'd love one.' She broke off suddenly with a slightly startled expression. 'I can't think why I should be telling you all this.

I suppose it's simply that I haven't met anyone — well, not anyone I could talk to since I've been back. But it must be shattering for you to have a complete stranger tell you her troubles.'

'You'd be surprised,' he remarked dryly as the barman slid a glass over to her. 'Cheers.'

'Cheers. Say — ' She was staring across the room. 'Is that someone looking for you?'

'Huh?'

'That girl.'

Craig momentarily nursed a guilty conscience. In the doorway Simone had just spotted them and was on her way over.

'Hallo.'

Simone cast a dispassionate eye on the blonde.

Craig introduced them. 'My secretary.'

The blonde held out a friendly hand. 'I'm Margaret Mason.'

She glanced swiftly from one to the other. 'Look,' she said, 'I think I'd better be running upstairs and see if that aunt of mine is showing any signs of life yet.'

'You haven't finished your drink.'

'Haven't I? Well, thanks for everything. But I really must get along.'

'Sit down,' said Craig. 'Finish your drink — then we'll go up with you.'

She looked at him curiously. 'But no. I couldn't let you do that. There's no need at all.'

'But yes.'

'But I mean, why on earth should you?'

'Just in case,' Craig said firmly.

She laughed unsteadily.

'But this is ridiculous. In case of what?'

'Drink your drink and don't talk so much.'

Margaret Mason looked helplessly at Simone.

'Does he always go on like this?'

'Always,' Simone assured her.

Craig said, 'If you're ready, let's be moving.'

Margaret Mason shrugged as if she couldn't care less and made her way through the now-crowded bar towards the vestibule and lifts. On their way, Simone whispered:

'A client?'

Craig looked down at her. 'Could be,'

he said cryptically.

Simone glanced at him swiftly. Something in his tone suggested that Craig had an idea that this girl might be more than a client. Maybe the principal player in — what?

Simone transferred her scrutiny to Margaret Mason, but her face was a mask. And, Simone decided regretfully, you couldn't help liking her with features and colouring like that, and the air of candour and friendliness that seemed to envelop her. A pity if she should turn out to be crooked. Simone's suspicions came to an abrupt halt as the lift stopped at the second floor.

'Here we are.'

Margaret Mason stepped out of the lift ahead of them, and as the gates clanged a middle-aged maidservant came out of one of the rooms along the corridor.

The girl said over her shoulder, in a flurry:

'I'll just ask the maid if she has been into my aunt's room yet. I inquired about it this morning.'

The maid halted as the girl approached

her and, with a passive face, stared at her.

'Good evening — ' the girl began.

'If you're going to ask about Mrs. Harrington,' the maid said, 'it's no good, madam.'

'What do you mean?'

'I haven't been able to get into twenty all day. So I don't know what's happened to Mrs. Harrington, any more than I did this morning.'

The blonde said sharply:

'What are you talking about — you don't know what's happened to Mrs. Harrington? Nothing has happened to her.'

'No, madam. I only got the impression, that's all.'

The woman shut her lips firmly.

Craig looked from the impassive face to Margaret Mason.

'How are you so sure nothing has happened?' he asked.

'But — but what could have happened?'

He took out a cigarette.

'You were pretty worried yourself downstairs,' he reminded her.

'Yes.' She hesitated. 'But how could

— oh, this is ridiculous.'

Craig addressed the maid:

'Mrs. Harrington is an old lady, isn't she? Haven't you reported this to the manager?'

'No, sir. I have my work to do same as everybody else, and if Mrs. Harrington likes to stay locked in her room all day, that's not my business.'

'Do you think there is really something wrong?' the blonde asked, worriedly.

Craig shrugged.

'Maybe some effort ought to be made to find out.'

'All right,' she said wearily. 'I had better go through my room and see if I can waken her by way of the window.'

Craig stood very still for a minute, then he said half to himself, 'Window?'

He had followed her to the door of number twenty-one while he spoke. She had paused with the key of her room in her hand. She said:

'A balcony runs outside the windows on this floor. I didn't want to go out there earlier because I didn't want to disturb my aunt this morning.'

'You had all this afternoon to make yourself known to her.'

'I have been out all this afternoon,' she answered.

'Beg your pardon, madam.' It was the maid who spoke. 'There isn't any need for you to go breaking in. I have duplicate keys of all the rooms on this floor.'

'Why didn't you use them before?' Craig snapped.

'It isn't my place to go into rooms while they're occupied — and locked,' she said significantly. 'But if you're worried about Mrs. Harrington I s'pose we're justified in opening the door. That is,' she added, 'if you'll take the responsibility, sir.'

The blonde said quickly:

'It is my responsibility. 1 can easily find out by way of the balcony — ' She slanted a swift look up at Craig as he snapped:

'Open the door.'

Margaret Mason said breathlessly:

'I don't know if my aunt would like us to walk in — '

'About as much as she would like us snooping round her balcony,' Craig answered with an edge to his voice.

She shrugged.

'All right then — and you can do the explaining.'

The maid seemed to have trouble finding the right key from amongst the bunch she jangled in her hand. Then she fitted one in the lock, twisted it and marched quickly into the room. Almost simultaneously she drew back.

Craig was already there, with the blonde and Simone crossing in after him.

On the rumpled unmade bed lay a frail, white-haired figure in a dressing gown. A loosely-knitted shawl had fallen half away from her shoulders. She was sprawling diagonally across the mattress, one hand flung limply over the edge.

Simone was the first to speak.

'She's been strangled.'

Margaret Mason sagged into a chair and buried her face in her hands.

Craig's eyes were flicking over the room and its contents. He moved over to the dressing table which stood by the window. On it was littered a variety of objects, not the least interesting being a heavy old-fashioned leather-covered jewel case. It was gaping and empty.

The maid's voice hit a hysterical note as her eyes followed Craig.

'She's been robbed! The murderer must have come in through the window. It's wide open.'

Craig stepped through the window on to the balcony and looked over the small parapet. A narrow side street ran below. Nothing on the street except a stray dog searching amongst bits of vegetable that littered the gutter.

Craig looked the balcony over. Only three bedrooms opened on to it. Numbers nineteen, twenty and twenty-one, he worked them out to be. Slowly he returned to the room. His eyes were narrowed but he said nothing.

The maid was gazing at Margaret Mason.

'Did Mrs. Mason, by any chance, go on to the balcony for some air?' she suggested.

The blonde dropped her hands from her face and stared at the other angrily. 'And just what do you mean by that?'

'Nothing.' The maid's tone was sour as a lemon. 'Only, madam, that you would have noticed if this window was open or not earlier in the day. Or last night.'

'I don't know what you are trying to insinuate. But I never went out on to the balcony at all. If you think — '

Craig cut in coldly:

'Nobody thinks anything, Mrs. Mason. I happen to know.'

His words fell like chips of ice. In the silence he walked over to the door and closed it. Then he turned the key in the lock. When he swivelled round again there was a slight smile playing round the corners of his mouth.

Margaret Mason turned wide staring eyes upon him.

'What are you doing?' she whispered. '*What are you doing?* I don't know anything about all this. I don't, I swear to you I don't. I've told you — '

'I know it.'

For the second time Craig's voice rasped across her words, then Simone caught the mildness in his tone as he went on: 'I believe you.'

Craig turned to Simone.

'Get on to the manager.'

As she crossed to the telephone, he whipped round on the maid.

'Would you rather tell us, or the police, where you have put the jewels?'

'Me?' the woman goggled at him.

'That's what I said.'

'I don't know what you're talking about.'

Craig sighed.

'You can't have any idea how tired I get of people not understanding me. Here it is then, in words of one or two syllables. You killed the old lady when she woke up and disturbed you in the act of pinching her sparklers. Get me?'

The woman's face contorted.

'I'm not admitting anything,' she yelled. 'However clever you talk, you can't frighten me into saying things you want me to say. And you can't prove anything either!'

'No?'

'You heard me,' the other said defiantly. 'Go on, then, go ahead and try. It's like I said it was, an outside job.'

116

Craig said:

'What you really mean is, that's what you hoped it would look — like an outside job.'

'Prove it,' she spat at him.

'Here's the story,' Craig went on unperturbed. 'As I have already said, you came in here to pinch the jewels and the old lady woke. You had to silence her somehow and the simplest way seemed to you to choke the screams back. Well you effectively did that. Then you opened the window to make it look like an outside job and sneaked out, locking the door after you.'

'And your proof?'

Craig touched the lock of the door.

'Here,' he said. 'You didn't have much trouble unlocking this door this morning, did you? A quite remarkable feat, really, if your story had been true.'

The maid had her hands to her throat. She made a queer strangled noise. Simone moved forward as the woman slid to the floor.

'Don't worry,' Craig told her. 'She's only fainted. I don't think there will be any trouble when the police arrive. Did you get on to the manager?'

She nodded.

'He's on his way. Just as soon as he has got through to Scotland Yard.'

Craig nodded.

'Now, take Mrs. Mason down to the bar and buy her a drink. When I've given the cops a welcoming party and handed over Unconscious, I'll join you. Have one ready.'

He found them, half an hour later, back where they had begun the evening, in the American bar. The blonde was saying:

'I still don't understand a word of it.'

Craig grinned at her. As he ordered more drinks Margaret Mason said:

'I realize it was that dreadful maid, but how you spotted her, I don't know.'

'What don't you understand?' Craig said.

'I thought you'd put the finger on me,' Margaret Mason went on shakily.

'I did — at first,' Craig said. 'You had such a perfect motive and opportunity.'

'What made you change your mind?'

'The key.'

Simone said:

'I know that. You told the maid. And she seemed to understand you. But we didn't.'

'Hers was the quick catch-on that goes with a guilty conscience. When she opened the door for us to go into the room, she went in ahead of us — remember? So she could return the key on the inside. She locked the door from outside last night, but she wanted it to look like an inside job. Only — if the key had been in the keyhole on the inside, as she wanted me to believe — she couldn't have used her duplicate this evening.'

He grinned and tipped the water-jug over Margaret Mason's glass.

She covered it with her hand.

'No thanks,' she said hurriedly. 'I'll take the darned stuff neat.'

8

The Woman with Moonlight Hair

Craig stood by the window of his office, gazing down into the street and at the opulent-looking limousine parked by the kerb.

'Does that belong to her?' he asked Simone, nodding down at the car.

'Yes. And I'd say she had plenty of money to go with it.'

Craig sighed.

'I thought I was going to have a peaceful morning. Did she say what was on her mind?'

Simone shook her head.

'But she's bothered. Beautiful and bothered. Her name is Mrs. Lansdowne.' She eyed him inquiringly. 'Mean anything to you?'

'Not a thing. Send her in.'

Mrs. Lansdowne was a tall, statuesque blonde wearing expensive furs, jewels and perfume plus an anxious expression. Pretty — and pretty dumb, he thought.

He switched on his smile and offered her a chair.

'Good morning, Mrs. Lansdowne. What's the worry?'

Her smile was a trifle wan.

'Quite a lot, I'm afraid. Do you think I could have a cigarette? I came without any.'

'I know how that can feel.'

He pushed the cigarette box on the desk over to her and gave her a light. The fact that her beautifully-kept hand was trembling didn't escape him.

'You needed that,' he observed.

She took a long, deep drag at her cigarette and expelled the smoke slowly.

'This whole ghastly business is getting on my nerves.'

Craig leaned back in his chair. He remembered not to put his feet up on the desk. 'Suppose you relax, and tell me all about it,' he suggested. 'You're among friends.'

She smiled at him.

'It's very nice of you to put it like that.

It's just that — well — I suppose I don't quite know where to begin.'

He answered lazily:

'When a beautiful woman is being blackmailed it usually begins round about the time she meets the blackmailer.'

'How — how did you know?'

Her question was tinged with suspicion. He congratulated himself on the success of his shot in the dark. He said easily:

'Merely a sample of the Master Mind at work. I haven't been tapping your telephone wires, so you can take it easy. Why else would a woman like you call on a man like me, unless it was over some little thing it would be better for your husband not to know about?'

'It sounds horrible, but — '

Craig cut in smoothly:

'I can tell you more. You've probably had a letter or a phone call this morning, threatening you that unless you pay up, your — er — friend, will spill the beans to your husband.'

She nodded slowly and he went on:

'That's what decided you to come to me for help.'

She stared at him helplessly.

'But — but how do you know all this?'

He grinned.

'You were in such a hurry you didn't bother to phone for an appointment. And you even forgot your cigarettes. Now relax and let's have the details. When did you first meet the blackmailer and how?'

She said weakly:

'You take my breath away.' He grinned at her. She said: 'Up to a point you're quite right. It is blackmail, in a kind of way, but not — not — '

'The way I indicated?'

'I haven't got mixed up with — with some man, or anything like that,' she said hurriedly. 'My husband and I are very happily married.'

Craig said:

'That's how it should be.' He spoilt it by adding cynically: 'Though if every husband and wife were, I should lose a lot of business.'

She drew nervously at her cigarette.

'I'd better start by explaining that I have quite a reputation for a fondness for jewellery. About a week ago a Mr.

Sylvester called to see me. He said he was a dealer in antique jewellery in a private way, and he had apparently heard of me through a firm with whom I've dealt quite a lot in the past. He offered me a pendant and I fell for it on the spot. I always do. But this pendant was something special and also had the advantage of being exactly what I wanted to wear with a new frock that evening at a party. Sylvester wanted three hundred pounds for it — it really was a bargain at the price — only I hadn't got that amount on me. You see, my husband makes me an allowance, which he pays into my bank every quarter. I'd nearly used it up.'

She stopped and gave him a veiled look through her long lashes.

'Go on,' he prompted her.

'Sylvester also wanted to be paid in cash.'

'Not the trusting type, eh?'

She drew one glove nervously through her other hand.

'He just said he preferred it that way. It — it seemed all right and I asked him if he would take fifty pounds cash and an

IOU for the remainder, with my promise to send him an open cheque within seven days. It was all I could do, and I did want that pendant.' She smiled ruefully. 'Anyway, he agreed to accept my proposal.'

'Accommodating of him.'

'Three days ago, I sent him the money, as agreed, and I naturally thought that was the end of it.'

'But,' said Craig, 'you were mistaken.'

'Horribly mistaken,' she admitted. 'This morning I had a letter from him.'

He waited while she fumbled in her handbag and drew out a long white envelope and, extracting a folded sheet of paper, handed it to him.

He spread it out and his eyes travelled rapidly down the typewritten letter.

'Dear Madam,

I am extremely surprised not to have received your cheque for £250 (Two hundred and fifty pounds), namely the balance outstanding for the pendant purchased by you last week.

I am sure you will recall your promise to pay this by today's date, and I am equally sure you will recall that I hold your IOU accordingly.

Unless I receive settlement by return, I shall be forced to draw your husband's attention to your IOU.'

It was signed in a thin flowery hand by Sylvester.

'Succinct, not to say somewhat sinister,' Craig murmured. 'I suppose you chatted freely to Sylvester about not wanting your husband to know?'

She drooped her head.

'Yes,' she admitted.

'And you think your husband wouldn't understand?'

Her eyes flew back to his face in alarm.

'Is that all you are going to tell me to do? I'm frightened of telling him because — oh, well, if you must know — I've been rather careless with money in the past. What I mean is, if he found out about this, it would upset him very much. And, it isn't as if I hadn't paid,' she added. 'I phoned my bank as soon as I got that horrible letter this morning and they said the cheque was cashed yesterday. Definitely.'

'You surprise me,' Craig commented dryly.

She fluttered one hand expressively.

'I tried to telephone Sylvester this morning, but there was no reply.'

Craig nodded thoughtfully and drummed on the desk with her folded letter.

'You think he is the greedy type? Not satisfied with the two-fifty he has already got, he's trying to soak you for it twice over?'

'I don't know what to think.'

He snapped out of his reverie and smiled at her.

'It wouldn't surprise me if you were right in thinking just that. As for your husband being upset, it would upset him even more if he still had to pay up that two-fifty.'

'I know,' she said miserably. 'That's why I came to you, Mr. Craig, can't you do something about it? Couldn't you prove in some way that this Sylvester monster has got, and did cash, my cheque?'

'Now, wait a minute. We can't take it conclusively he's a crook, even though it looks that way at the moment.'

'He must be. What else can have happened?'

He looked at her steadily.

'You're not giving me much to go on,' he said, tapping the ash off his cigarette. He looked at the letter again, and paused. 'However,' he conceded, 'we'll see what your pendant-hawker pal has got to say about it.'

'You mean you will help me?'

Craig smiled at the hope in her expression.

'For a very small fee. See my secretary on the way out. She will fix it up with you. I'll be getting in touch.'

'I can't thank you enough.'

'Don't be too hopeful,' he warned her as he opened the door to the outer office for her.

Sylvester's address was just off Berkeley Street and they arrived there early in the afternoon after an excellent lunch.

'Classy,' remarked Craig to Simone as they stood on the pavement gazing at the little shop. He pushed open the door and stood aside for Simone.

As the door closed behind them a wave

of exotic perfume trailed out to greet their nostrils.

The wearer of the subtle scent emerged from the shadows at the back of the shop. She was young and shapely, heavily but beautifully made up.

It was her hair that attracted attention. It was prematurely grey but she had been using a blue tint and the moonlight effect that glinted in it enhanced its charm above her youthful face. She wore something black in a sophisticated and miraculous cut which accentuated her svelte hips, and Simone gazed enviously at her sheer silk stockings. She glanced at Craig.

'Can I help you?'

The woman managed to infuse character into those shopworn words as she drew close to them.

'We were just looking round,' Craig said.

She smiled with great charm.

'Is there anything in which you are especially interested?'

Craig caught the nuance of invitation in her low voice though her wide-apart hazel eyes appraised him innocently.

Simone rose to her cue.

'I'm rather fond of antique jewellery,' she said in her attractive French accent.

'We have quite a lot at the moment, madam. One or two very lovely old rings.'

Craig murmured almost to himself.

'Not a ring. I'd suggest a pendant.'

'A pendant?' There was no hesitation in her voice at all. 'I'm not sure.'

'Something like the one Mrs. Lansdowne bought, for instance,' Craig went on chattily.

'Mrs. Lansdowne?'

Craig had the satisfaction of knowing he had, anyway, momentarily startled her out of her silky manner.

Then her eyes hardened.

'If you are a friend of Mrs. Lansdowne's,' she said in a brittle voice, 'I don't think Mr. Sylvester would be particularly glad to know it.'

'Oh?' Craig took out a cigarette. 'I'm disappointed.'

'So were we — in Mrs. Lansdowne.'

Through a puff of cigarette smoke Craig eyed the lovely sapphire clasp which she wore in her lapel, and which exactly matched her earrings.

'Would Mr. S. be in?' he asked softly.

'I'm afraid not.'

'We can wait,' said Craig comfortably.

The woman crossed to the door.

'I don't think Mr. Sylvester would be very pleased to see you,' she said coldly. 'So perhaps, under the circumstances, it would be better if you left.'

Craig raised his eyebrows.

'Of course,' he put forward, 'we could always be calling to pay over a cheque for Mrs. Lansdowne.'

'What?' She closed the door. 'Somehow I don't think you are.'

'No? Why not?'

'Mrs. Lansdowne said she would send the cheque. She did not. If she had decided to pay for the pendant she bought she would not have put it in the post after receiving Mr. Sylvester's letter, nor would she have entrusted it to someone else. She would have brought it in herself.'

'Very nicely put,' murmured Craig admiringly. 'I'll be frank with you, and admit I was playing for time. We're still waiting for the boss.'

An annoyed little smile crossed her face.

'I have already told you, I am in charge here. Mr. Sylvester spends most of his time calling on clients. He has quite an extensive — '

She broke off as the shop door opened and a thick-set, pudgy character in a light suit entered. 'Here is Mr. Sylvester,' she said, 'if you insist on seeing him.' And she shrugged and turned away as if she washed her hands of the whole business.

Sylvester closed the door quietly behind him and switched an expansive smile on Simone from behind a long cigar.

'Good afternoon,' he purred. 'I hope you are finding something that pleases you!'

It was Craig who spoke:

'That depends.'

'On what, sir? I assure you we will do our best to help you in any way.'

Craig smiled back at him.

'That makes it a lot easier. First of all, your assistant here doesn't think we ought to mention the fact we are friends of Mrs. Lansdowne.'

Sylvester's suave smile was wiped off his face like chalk off a blackboard. His rather small, over-bright eyes glittered.

'Mrs. Lansdowne is not one of my favourite customers.'

'Pity. The more so, because she happens to be my client.'

'Your client?'

Behind Sylvester the woman swung round and stared hard at Craig.

Craig gazed at Sylvester tranquilly.

'I am a private detective,' he said. 'The name is Craig.'

'So you've come snooping round my shop,' Sylvester squealed. 'Trying to prove I'm attempting to force her into paying twice over.'

Craig said smoothly:

'You appear to have misunderstood me. My client merely wants me to prove that she sent you her cheque.'

'Well, she's a liar,' Sylvester said angrily. 'She owes me two hundred and fifty pounds, and she's not going to get away with it. Even if she has hired a detective to try and scare me off.'

'You've got — '

Craig was interrupted by the woman, who had come forward holding a small

Buddha in one hand and twisting it idly between her fingers. Her manner had entirely altered and she flashed a friendly smile at him.

'I've never met a detective before,' she announced disarmingly.

Sylvester swung round on her.

'Chloe,' he said, 'have we, or have we not, received any cheque from Mrs. Lansdowne?'

She replied, still with her engaging smile.

'Certainly not, Mr. Sylvester.' She turned to Craig. 'I'm afraid Mrs. Lansdowne must be suffering from well — shall we say, hallucinations?' She paused, raising her evebrows ingratiatingly. 'If she insists that she sent it to us it might of course, be lost in the post.'

Her tone indicated that it was the last thing she thought had happened.

Craig nodded, saying softly:

'The cheque has been cashed at her bank. Or didn't you know?'

Sylvester appeared slightly taken aback.

'Is — is that so? No, I didn't know it had been. Cashed at her bank.' As he repeated the words he massaged his chin with the back of his podgy hand. 'I must admit it looks as if she posted it, in that case.'

'Does look like that, doesn't it?' agreed Craig.

Sylvester eyed him narrowly as a further thought came to him. 'And she thinks I cashed it?'

Before Craig could answer the woman called Chloe slanted a look up at him from beneath her heavy lashes.

'I deal with all accounts,' she said. 'Perhaps you would care to accompany me to the bank.'

Craig smiled and took time to reply.

'If you deal with the accounts, perhaps that would be a good idea.'

She smiled back at him.

'There's a branch just around the corner. You can ask them whether I cashed that particular cheque. But I'm afraid, although I shall enjoy the walk, I can assure you here and now that you will be wasting your time — so far as your client is concerned,' she added archly.

Sylvester broke in worriedly:

'I think it is a good idea, Mr. Craig. I don't like any of this business at all, and I should be only too happy to clear up the situation. Why don't you go along with her?'

'Because,' said Craig, 'she's much too smart.'

The woman wasn't quite sure whether to take this as a compliment or not.

'What do you mean?'

'Much too smart,' went on Craig, eyeing her, 'to cash the cheque right on your doorstep.'

Simone, who had been watching and waiting as the atmosphere grew tenser, gasped: 'How — ?'

'Are you accusing me?' the woman said dangerously.

Craig grinned at her bleakly.

'You see,' he said, 'if you had never seen Mrs. Lansdowne's cheque, how do you know there's a branch of her bank just around the corner?'

'Chloe!' It was Sylvester who shattered the silence that ensued.

Under her make-up the woman's face was ashen.

'I — ' she began and the Buddha she had been holding slipped from her nerveless fingers and crashed to the floor.

'You crook,' shouted Sylvester, lunging at her as if he intended to strike her. 'You dirty little thieving — !'

Craig eyed the shattered fragments of the Buddha. He said:

'And I shouldn't let her kid you that came to pieces in her hands either.'

9

The Man in the Summer House

Barbara Drummond had got everything.

This added up to a creamy complexion, a goddess-like head, and a lithe young figure with long legs. But the most enchanting feature about her was her eyes. Deep-set and slanting, they were a colour nobody could successfully define. Sometimes a slate blue with dark hyacinth flecks, or grey with amber lights, or — when she wore emerald — they were green. Whatever their colour anyway, they were always intriguing. Then there was her flaming golden-red hair, which she wore straight and long to her shoulders. Somehow too she always managed to use a lipstick that was exactly right and accentuated her wide laughing mouth to the delight and despair of any and every young man around.

Added to which, Barbara Drummond had money. Plenty.

This didn't mean she was a Bond Street doll. She wore her clothes with a sort of careless indifference that was in itself perfection.

It was at a party Craig first met her.

She was wearing white and a couple of gardenias clipped into the loose wave in her hair. Craig liked pretty women as well as the next man, maybe more so. Almost as much anyhow as he detested parties. He had only attended this one because it was being given by Sir Gregory and Lady Dawlish and, having once cleared up a little case of blackmail for Lady Dawlish by the simple expedient of impersonating her husband, he had been unable to resist the temptation of meeting the man whose place he had taken on that occasion.

Now, having said 'Hallo' he was just beginning to think it was going to be as boring as any other, when he saw somebody else he knew. He walked across the room and tapped Bruce Kershaw on the shoulder.

'Mr. Craig.'

'Hush,' responded Craig mock-mysteriously. 'Sir Gregory would hate to think he was entertaining a detective — however private he might be.'

Bruce Kershaw laughed.

'I'm glad to meet you unprofessionally,' he said. 'I thought for one horrible moment we had a suspected malefactor amongst us.'

'Long words you use.' Craig cast a dispassionate eye over the room. 'On the contrary, pretty dull. How is Auntie?' he added with a twinkle in his eye.

'Well,' the other grimaced. 'And I am very respectable.'

'No gambling parties?'

'No gambling parties.'

Neither of them mentioned the sweet young piece Bruce Kershaw had once thought of as his bride-to-be. Margot Delling was even now where Craig had helped to put her, serving a sentence for a neat little jewel robbery that hadn't been neat enough.

'Did you say this party was dull? Look who's just come in.'

Craig looked.

'She's out of this world,' he admitted as the most lovely redhead he had ever seen stood in the doorway

Bruce Kershaw smiled.

'She's that — and more.'

'Who is she?'

'Barbara Drummond.' Bruce Kershaw turned to look at him. 'I'm going over.'

Craig thought it was sheer malice not to offer to introduce him to the delectable young woman.

It was La Drummond herself who had other ideas on this subject. A few minutes later she came over to him with Bruce Kershaw in tow.

Introductions over, they somehow managed to lose Kershaw. For the remainder of the evening Craig found her the most entertaining girl he'd met for a long time, Eventually he took her home to her guardian's big house in Richmond in a taxi.

She hadn't talked much about herself, and thinking back afterwards he realized just how little she had told him. Perhaps that was part of her charm. Anyway it was refreshing to Craig who normally spent his life listening to other people's life stories. All he learnt of Barbara Drummond's personal history was that she was the adopted daughter of a man called Laurie whom she adored.

Two weeks after the Dawlish party he met Bruce Kershaw by accident in Oxford Street. They shook hands and the former asked him to join him for a drink. It was rather an abrupt invitation, but the other was very young and Craig was well aware he was regarded as some sort of hero in Bruce Kershaw's eyes.

They went into a bar and Bruce Kershaw ordered the round.

Presently Craig asked casually:

'Seen Barbara Drummond lately?'

The colour that mounted rapidly to the roots of the other's unruly hair gave Craig his answer.

'Well, yes, I have.' He grinned and added awkwardly: 'Matter of fact, I've been seeing quite a lot of her — small thanks to you.'

'A very charming girl.'

'Yes, isn't she? She talks a lot of you. She thought you were pretty nice — unfortunately.'

Craig laughed.

'You've got nothing to worry about,' he said.

Bruce Kershaw frowned.

'I'm a bit worried about her, to tell the

142

truth. She isn't very happy.'

Craig's surprise was genuine. He said:

'I thought she was one of the world's happier people.'

'She was. But her guardian's daughter has turned up again after two years.'

'Didn't know he had one.'

The boy nodded. He was still frowning.

'Funny girl. Afraid there isn't much love lost between Barbara and Lyn.'

'Lyn?'

'The daughter. Name's Evelyn really, but she is always called Lyn. I gather she is making trouble between the old man and Barbara. There was some sort of a row soon after Barbara first went to live there, which was why Lyn left. I don't know much about it, you know what Barbara is, hates worrying other people with her troubles. But I'm afraid there will be a major bust-up soon.'

'Too bad,' murmured Craig.

They dropped the subject after that, and Craig gave Barbara Drummond and her worries little more thought. But, as with greatness, some people have cases thrust upon them, and this case was destined to be just one of those.

A few days after his meeting with Bruce Kershaw the telephone on his desk jangled.

It was Barbara Drummond.

'Can I come and see you?'

'I'd love it.'

When she arrived she was looking as breathlessly lovely as ever.

'Bruce told me who you were,' she said and smiled. 'You were so sweet last time I met you. When I heard you were a detective, I thought you were the very person I ought to come and see.'

'Detective or no detective,' Craig told her, 'I am the very person. What's the trouble?'

'Nothing very tangible.'

She shook her head as he offered her a cigarette. 'No thanks, I don't smoke much you know.'

He lit his cigarette while she went on, looking up at him from eyes that today were hyacinth-flecked.

'I think Bruce has told you a little. Two months ago Mr. Laurie's daughter — his real daughter — came home. She is about five years older than I. Originally they had had some sort of silly quarrel. Well, not a quarrel really. It was a bad row, I don't know the exact ins and outs, Daddy (Craig remembered she called her guardian that) would never talk of her afterwards. But she walked out on him.'

'And they never saw each other again until two months ago?'

She shook her head.

'When they did, she put over the prodigal daughter act. You know the sort of thing, it made me sick. And what makes me so furious now is that Daddy, being the dear, kindly, believing old darling he is, was completely taken in.'

Craig got up and walked round behind her chair.

'So? There's something more to all this, or you wouldn't have come to me. I'm not a kind of family guardian angel.'

She said:

'It isn't very easy to say. Now I'm here I don't know what you can do about it anyway.'

'Tell me,' he said quietly. 'Even if I can do nothing. I like to hear you talk.'

She glanced swiftly up at him with a faint smile.

'You're a dear,' she told him softly.

He raised his brows and grinned.

'Some other time,' he said. 'This is business.'

'It's just that Daddy has been ill ever since Lyn arrived back,' she said slowly. 'I am terribly worried about him really. He seems to be failing so much and he is so depressed. I can't do anything with him.'

'Tried getting the doctor in?'

'Of course. He says it's his heart and high blood pressure. That's what worries me. There isn't a day goes by without Lyn flying into one of her rages. It upsets him dreadfully and he seems to get weaker after each quarrel. Honestly, I think it will kill him if she stays in the house much longer.' She took Craig's arm. 'Isn't there anything you can do to get her away?'

Craig covered her hand with his.

'Afraid I can't just remove people from their own homes by force if they don't want to go. Can't you get him away for a month or so? Leave this girl behind?'

'I've tried that, but he won't hear of it.

He adores his house by the river. He has got a sort of thing about the river. Poor Daddy,' she added softly, almost as if she had forgotten Craig was there. 'He is so sentimental.'

A little smile played round her lips.

Craig said:

'What is the real trouble between Lyn and her father?'

She looked at him. A wary light suddenly came into those wonderful eyes of hers.

'I don't know,' she said guardedly.

'You know,' he told her, 'but you aren't prepared to tell me.'

'You're making a mistake, I don't know.'

Craig looked down at her then he shrugged.

'I can't help you, if you won't tell me,' he said. 'If you change your mind, you know where to reach me.'

That was all there was to it.

When she had gone he rang up Bruce Kershaw, but he knew less than Craig. It seemed he had only met Lyn once and hadn't been very struck. Craig decided to forget the whole thing.

A week went by before he heard from her again. The telephone rang in his office about five o'clock. He picked it up and her voice hummed in his ear. He thought it sounded shaky.

'Could you come over here?'

'Right now?'

'Please. It's Daddy. He — he's dead.'

He told her tersely:

'I'm on my way.'

Some forty minutes later his taxi drew up outside the front gates of her house. He paid off the driver and went quickly up the short well-kept drive, the lawn spreading itself smoothly away to the right down to the river.

It was Bruce Kershaw who answered his knock on the front door.

'Thank God you're here.'

'She said she was alone.'

'She rang me immediately she had finished talking to you. I came straight away.'

Barbara Drummond appeared at that moment in the doorway of the lounge. She was white and looked shaken. Craig went over to her at once.

'What happened?'

'It's suicide,' she answered simply. 'Daddy committed suicide.'

He eyed her for a moment narrowly.

'Have you phoned the police?'

Bruce had come up behind them.

'She wouldn't let me,' he told Craig, 'until you arrived.'

'I thought you would know best what to do,' she said.

Craig looked at Bruce Kershaw.

'Get on to the police now.' Then he said to the girl:

'Where is he and how did it happen? Try and tell me all about it.'

'He is in the summer house down by the river, I — I found him — '

'How did he do it?' Craig persisted.

'He was taking some tablets — they were dangerous I know — and he took an overdose.'

Craig looked at her thoughtfully. It would be better, he thought, if she could break down and cry.

Bruce Kershaw came back from telephoning.

'I got on to them. They're coming along right away.'

'Where's the daughter?' Craig asked.

He shrugged.

'I don't know. I don't know any more about any of this than you do. She was here and then she went — ' he broke off and placed a protecting arm round the girl's shoulders

Craig nodded thoughtfully. He said:

'All right. Let's take a look at the summer house.'

Mechanically she led the way, clinging to Bruce Kershaw's arm, through the French windows out on to the terrace. Down the shallow steps and across the lawn towards the river.

Half hidden by flowering trees and facing the glinting water was the summer house. It was large and well built. More of a bungalow, thought Craig. On its wooden planking there was a table and a large wicker armchair

The silvery-haired figure, lying back with his head against the cushions, seemed to all appearances peacefully asleep. On the table in front if him stood a glass and a large empty bottle. Pinned by the bottle, and lifting every now and then in the breeze that came off the water, was a single sheet of paper.

Craig turned to the girl.

'Did you come down here with him today?'

She nodded.

'He had been having a sleeping draught in the afternoons and he liked me to mix it for him. I did it this afternoon as usual. I suppose he must have added the rest of the tablets when I had gone.'

'You left the bottle on the table?'

'I suppose I did.' She brushed her hand across her forehead. 'I don't really remember, but I suppose I must have.'

Craig indicated the sheet of paper on the table.

'Have you read it?'

'Yes. But I didn't touch it. I didn't touch anything, because I knew the police — anyway, he must have written it and then taken the rest of the tablets.'

Craig glanced at the bottle. It was labelled in red: Poison. And something about sticking rigidly to the prescribed amount. Then he leaned over and read the shaky handwriting.

'Goodbye beautiful river. I feel so tired I can't go on. So I say farewell to life and all who are dear to me knowing they will understand, in the loveliest spot I know.'

As he straightened up again, Craig remarked:

'Seems to have been a little eccentric.'

That was putting it mildly, he felt. The note, anyway, seemed definitely pretty sentimental.

'What does it say?'

It was Bruce Kershaw who put the query.

Craig nodded for him to read it for himself. The girl was saying:

'He had been ill and his nerves were bad. That's all. Then Lyn got him down so much I suppose he didn't feel he could go on any more. It's as good as if she killed him.'

Craig said slowly:

'Try not to worry about that. Where is she now?'

'She went over to some friends. She left

about nine thirty this morning. It was going to be such a lovely day. The servants have the afternoon off and Daddy and I were going to be alone for once.'

Craig's eyes narrowed.

'Sure she's been away for the day?'

'Of course. She telephoned at about three o' clock she wouldn't be back til supper tonight.'

'Speak to anyone else where she was phoning from?'

She thought a moment. Then:

'Yes. But — '

'Looks like she was there all right,' Craig murmured.

Bruce Kershaw started to say:

'You mean that Lyn — you thought —?' he broke off and followed Craig's gaze. He was eyeing a large portrait on the wall of the summer house. It was the picture of a sulky-mouthed brunette with a rebellious air about her.

'That,' Craig murmured, 'would be her?'

'Yes,' Barbara Drummond said.

Craig's gaze returned to the lovely red-head and there was a puzzled look in his eyes.

'Was your guardian's handwriting affected by his illness?' he asked.

'It was pretty shaky. As you can see. I told you these last few weeks have been so dreadful for him.'

Craig lit a cigarette, frowning.

Somewhere, somehow, there was something wrong. He had missed out somewhere along the line, and he didn't like it. His eyes flicked over the table again.

'What's the matter?' asked Bruce Kershaw, watching furiously.

Craig didn't answer.

He had begun to search the floor of the summer house. He went over the floor inch by inch. When he was satisfied that what he was looking for was not there, he started on the small gravel path that ran in front. Kershaw and the girl looked on in puzzled silence.

Then Craig straightened up. He said to the girl:

'Sure you've been alone all the afternoon?'

'Look here, Craig, what is all this?' Bruce Kershaw said.

Craig threw him a glance and then

turned his attention to the dead man's pockets, emptying the contents on to the table. A watch, handkerchief, lighter, cigarette case, wallet, some small change and a bunch of keys.

'What the devil are you looking for?'

Craig turned back to Bruce Kershaw. 'The missing link,' he said grimly. 'And it isn't there.'

Barbara Drummond stepped forward and whispered, 'But it's suicide, isn't it?'

There was a moment's silence before Craig answered.

'It's murder.'

'Murder!' Bruce Kershaw exclaimed. 'But this is horrible. Who would want to — besides who had the opportunity? You must be mistaken.'

'I'm not mistaken,' said Craig.

'But no one had the opportunity, I'm telling you.'

Craig didn't bat an eyelash.

'No, no one had the opportunity.'

Barbara Drummond was silent, staring at him. Then she said, her voice so low it was almost inaudible:

'No one had the opportunity. Except — '

Craig said slowly:

'It couldn't have been anyone else.'

Bruce Kershaw was glancing from one to the other. He was utterly mystified, but something about the tenseness of the atmosphere stopped him from butting in.

'No,' the girl breathed. '*No!*'

Craig said quietly:

'Why?'

Barbara Drummond suddenly buried her face in her hands and sobbed.

Bruce Kershaw stared at her; his face was contorted with disbelief.

'I don't believe it. I just don't believe it — Craig, there must be some mistake.'

'She murdered her guardian.'

Craig's voice was stony, but there was a haggard look round his eyes. 'Poisoned him when he asked her to mix his sleeping draught, then she wrote the note. It looked a good suicide — except for the missing link. Obviously it had been written right here, but she forgot to add to the table decorations a pen and ink, nor had her guardian a fountain pen. It had to be murder. *And there was no one else.*'

Barbara Drummond raised her head. Craig noticed in a detached manner that he couldn't have described the colour of her eyes for a million pounds.

She looked straight at him.

'You needn't worry,' she said, 'that I'll mind you calling the police. I don't mind the police. Now.'

It was Craig who caught on and got to her first. She shook herself free.

'Leave me alone. You see, that was a full bottle of tablets. I didn't give them all to Daddy, I kept some. You thought I was crying just now. I wasn't. I took the rest of the tablets. Daddy was a sentimental old man. He was going to divide his money between us.' Her eyes turned to the brunette's picture on the wall. 'Between Lyn and me. Why should she get any of his money? It should have all come to me. To me. That was why I had to stop him altering his will somehow. I had to kill him — '

She broke off in a strangled gasp, her hand at her throat. Her eyelids drooped and she swayed.

Craig caught her as she started to slide to the floor, and her long golden-red hair made a violent splash of colour on his coat.

10

The Wimbledon Common Clue

Mike Pearce was feeling somewhat peeved.

He had cause to be, he argued. It was hard enough, after living a life that had not been as exactly straight as the traditional die to keep one's feet from wandering from the horny path of virtue and honesty, without being unfairly suspected of a crime of which he was not guilty.

Decidedly and definitely not guilty. Not this time.

It was thus that he whiningly expressed himself to Craig round about twelve o'clock one morning. He had shuffled straight from the police's nosy questionings into his personal life and habits, to Craig's office. Craig, like the police, knew Mike Pearce of old, and, like the police, was inclined to be sceptical of his story.

However, here Mike Pearce was, blinking owlishly at Craig from under his drooping eyelids and rolling a dirty fag end round and round in a sort of wet monotony on his lower lip.

'Look,' said Mike Pearce with some bitterness, 'here have I bin for the last five year, honest as the day, struggling, Mr. Craig, struggling to keep me and my missus going on wot we picks up from them old antiques, keeping my nose clean and avoiding coppers like they was the mumps, and wot should happen? We gets wrongfully and wilfully accused of something wot we hadn't anythink to do with. Is it right, Mr. Craig? 'Course it ain't.'

Craig shook his head in agreement.

He was quite fascinated by the other's cigarette manoeuvres and began to wonder whether or not the cigarette end was a permanent feature of Mike Pearce's lower lip.

'It ain't easy,' Mike Pearce pointed out. 'It never has bin easy going, but we've managed with scraping here and scratching there, and keeping straight. All the time, keeping straight. That's how my missus wanted it when I comes out last time, five years ago. 'Straight, Mike . . . '

Them were the words she used. 'You gotter go straight or else I'll be leaving you.' That's wot she said, and straight I bin ever since. But where does it git yer? Into this sort of a mess, that's where.'

Craig gathered that antique dealing in Streatham was not, from the cash angle, anyway, on a par with the 'fence' business. Mike Pearce looked as if he might keep up his air of aggrieved righteousness indefinitely without ever coming any nearer to the point. So Craig decided it was about time he got the full story.

'I take it,' he said, 'you've had a visit from the police. Exactly what do they think you're responsible for?'

'A little job down Wimbledon way. There's a house down there wot had a good many bits and pieces of valuable objects of art, as you might say, and somebody gone and swiped 'em — so they tell me,' he added hurriedly. ''Course, I didn't know a thing about it till they told me. Leastways, I didn't know where the stuff had come from, honest.'

Craig eyed him narrowly.

'But you knew they were stolen goods, eh?'

Mike Pearce looked surprised.

'Well, I'm getting ter that, ain't I?'

'I was wondering.'

'Somebody,' stated Mike Pearce plaintively, 'planted it on me. And that's a dirty trick, if ever there was one!'

'So the police actually found the stuff on you?'

'Now Mr. Craig, you got it all wrong. I *gave* the junk ter the police, soon as I found it. Thought I'd be doing 'em a good turn. And wot do them flatfeet do, but turn right round on a chap and all for doing his dooty as an honest citizen.'

'Let's get this right,' Craig said patiently. 'As I see it, for the last five years you have been running an antique shop in Streatham that isn't doing terrific business but keeps you out of jail. Some character — according to you, unknown — pinched some valuable antiques from a house in Wimbledon, palmed them off on you without you knowing it, but when you recognized the stolen goods you took them to the police. Right?'

162

'S'right,' agreed Mike Pearce. 'Y'see, it was like this. I happened to be up in London yesterday. A young chap comes into the shop while I was gone and spins my missus a yarn about them being family heirlooms and all that. Tells her he wants to be rid of 'em 'cos he is going abroad see?'

Craig said he saw.

'She,' the other went on, 'not knowing nothing about it, gives him forty quid for the things, and pushes off. While it was happening I'd seen a description in the paper of the items wot were missing. When I gits home, there's some of them very items, large as life, in my shop. So wot do I do?'

'I can hardly wait — tell me.'

'I takes 'em straight off to the police, as I should. But I never knew anythink more about it, Mr. Craig sure as I sits here, I didn't.'

Mike Pearce rolled his fag end more fiercely than ever in protest.

Craig leaned back in his chair and surveyed him blandly.

'And the police just didn't believe the

stuff you took into them was the lot? They think that you palmed them off with a small percentage to clear yourself of suspicion whilst hanging on to the rest?'

The other nodded vehemently.

'That's it. Once you done wrong you can't never do right according to them. Nasty suspicious minds.'

'And what do you want me to do?'

'I wants yer to take up the case, Mr. Craig,' Mike Pearce said earnestly. 'Prove my innocence to them bleary-eyed lot down at the Yard, wot can't see an inch in front of their noses. You gotter, Mr. Craig, you're a lover of justice, and you wouldn't be put off by a chap having done time five year ago, would you now?' He took a breath, then: 'Wot d'yer say?'

Craig smiled sceptically.

But in the end he broke under Mike Pearce's inelegant but eloquent persistence. Reluctantly he finally said:

'I'll be down to see you this afternoon and have a chat with your wife.'

After Mike Pearce had departed, Simone put her head round the door.

'What a peculiar little man. Did you ring?'

Craig nodded, his feet on the desk.

'I shall be out this afternoon, if you'll take care of the customers this end.' He glanced across at her and grinned. 'When is a fence not a fence?' he demanded suddenly and irrelevantly.

She frowned.

'I do not understand?' she queried in charming bewilderment.

'Not something that runs round a garden,' he explained. 'A fence is a character who buys knocked-off goods.' He nodded towards the door. 'The cops think our late departed client seems to be well in the running under that heading.'

'And you?'

'I'm inclined to side with them, for all I promised Mike Pearce I'd take up the case in his favour.'

'But, if you side with the police in your theory about him, why do you do that?'

Craig smiled bleakly.

'He tells me,' he said, 'I am a lover of justice. He was so insistent, I simply couldn't refuse him.'

★ ★ ★

Later that afternoon he was standing outside 'M. Pearce, Antiques.'

He eyed some of the contents of the windows, plus various articles spread outside the shop on the pavement.

There was an old armchair that was generously distributing some of its horse-hair to the world for nothing; a rough wood table that had probably graced somebody's kitchen, but had since been heavily disguised by dark paint and varnish and was now described as a dark oak refectory table; and a heap of old brasses and china dogs.

Craig smiled and went inside.

Mike Pearce drew him into the musty little back parlour to meet the missus. The missus proved to be quite as voluble as her better half, with a naggingly shrill tongue.

She swept back a strand of greying hair from her thin face and scrutinized Craig with light shrewish eyes.

'So you're a private dick?'

Craig said he hoped he was.

'I told Mike he ought to be careful who he gets mixed up with. But there, he never takes a blind bit of notice of wot I say. And where does it land him?'

Craig interrupted her gently. 'Wasn't it you who bought his stolen stuff yesterday?'

He caught the grateful glance thrown him by Mike Pearce.

'And why?' Mrs. Pearce retorted. 'Because I'm kept in the dark about these things, that's why. How was I s'posed to know, seeing as I'm never allowed a say in what gets brought in and sent out of this place. Not that I'm not saying anything about him being dishonest, mind. He never had nothing to do with this robbery, and that's a fact.'

Craig managed to get the thin edge of a word in:

'Suppose you tell me what happened while your husband was out yesterday.'

'If Mike hadn't gone off when he ought to have been in the shop, this never would have happened,' she flared. 'Not that I know what he wanted to go to London for anyway. If you ask me, it was to go squandering his money where he didn't ought to, that's what I think — '

Craig took out a cigarette and tapped it on his case.

'I suppose you realize you're making things look worse for him with all this chat?'

She stared at him incredulously.

'I'm a good wife to him, I'll have you know. Who is it that's kept him the way he should go these last five years? Me. Who's worked and slaved and scrubbed and scraped, all for him? Me. And now who has the nerve to tell me I'm making things worse for him?'

'Me,' Craig said.

'Mr. Craig's tryin' to help,' whined Mike Pearce unhappily.

'You be quiet,' she snapped.

'Look,' Craig said, 'if you'll start where this character sold you this stolen stuff, maybe we'll get somewhere. Maybe.'

'Yesterday, about lunch time it was. He seemed genuine enough to me, and said he wanted the money quickly 'cos he was going abroad in the next day or two. And that's all there is to it. I bought it off him and didn't think no more about it, till Mike here comes home and had a look at it and sees what it is. But it was never my fault.'

'Can you describe him?'

As he asked the question Craig caught the worried look Mike Pearce shot at his wife.

'I'd say he was about thirty,' she said thoughtfully. 'Dark, he was, and got a thin face and thin lips too, that sort of twitched a bit as he was talking. Wore a proper nice smart overcoat, very tight-fitting.'

Craig looked across at Mike Pearce.

'That description mean a thing to you?'

'I wouldn't like to say anythink offhand, Mr. Craig,' the other began cautiously. 'I knowed some o' the boys in the old days, but that was a good bit ago. But when the missus told me about him, it did put me in mind of a chap called Fenley, he worked that line once.'

Craig eyed him narrowly.

'Fenley? The description certainly fits him nicely. If I remember rightly, he had quite an eye for collector's pieces. Got five years for that job at the Oriental Museum. I didn't know he was out.'

'No more did I.' Mike Pearce was anxious to please. ' 'Course if I'd bin in the shop, I'd 've spotted him and sent him packing. But, I told yer, Mr. Craig, 's'only an idea it could 've bin 'im.'

'Not a bad idea, at that. I believe I could put my hands on our friend, come to think.'

'I hopes you have some luck, Mr. Craig,' said Mrs. Pearce fervently. 'I do and all. If it's only ter put Mike in the clear.'

★ ★ ★

Back in his office Craig told Simone:
'We're going slumming.'

Their slumming took them to a flashy dive in a Mayfair mews, that got by under the name of 'The Last Laugh'.

The bird they sought was perched before the bar as if he had never left it since Craig had last seen him there, years back. 'The Last Laugh' was not one of Craig's favourite bars.

'Hallo, Fenley,' said Craig, leaning an

170

elbow on the counter at Fenley's side. 'It's been a long time.'

Fenley didn't appear to be unduly startled by Craig's sudden appearance.

'Evening, Mr. Craig. Rotten weather lately, ain't it?'

Craig agreed. From the weather they went on to the price of drink, the state of the country and other chitchat.

'Thought you were planning a little trip abroad?' said Craig presently, when he, Simone and Fenley had their drinks.

Fenley's lips twitched. 'Whatever in the world gave you that idea?'

Craig smiled pleasantly.

'Just a rumour I heard down Wimbledon way.'

Fenley laughed loud and long.

'Wimbledon? Now who would know what I was going to do at Wimbledon?'

'You tell me,' murmured Craig. 'Who?'

Fenley looked at him sideways.

'You suggesting anything?' he demanded suspiciously.

Craig answered blithely:

'Why? You heard about that little job too?'

Fenley thrust out his chin.

'I read the papers, same as others. But you wouldn't be thinking I had anything to do with that, would you?'

Craig spoke thoughtfully to the ceiling.

'They tell me,' he said, 'they are looking for a character the spit and image of you. Description that you'd fit like a glove.'

Instead of explosively denying it, as Simone, with some apprehension, was expecting him to do, Fenley remarked agreeably:

'I know the cops have been nosing around.' He grinned disarmingly. 'I'll let you in on that, since you know so much. But I'm in the clear. Miles and miles away from Wimbledon I was day that job was pulled. Brighton, s'matter of fact. Ever such a nice place, Brighton. Ever bin down that way, Mr. Craig? You?' He turned to Simone. 'You should go, ever such lovely fresh air.'

'What would you be doing in Brighton,' Craig said, 'besides breathing ozone?'

'All I was doing was seeing a chap. Old pal of mine. Nice to be able to see all one's old pals now and then. S'matter of fact,' he went on casually, 'this chap backed my alibi.'

Craig smiled at him.

'Nice to have a pal like that.'

'I'll say.' Fenley winked broadly. 'But it's honest, Mr. Craig, strike me if it ain't. Y'see, I happen to have taken to the straight and narrer these days. Not worth going crooked, frankly.'

'I like you best when you're frank.' The other chuckled. Craig said: 'Like your old pal, Pearce.'

Fenley blinked. Then he said rapidly:

'Pearce? Never heard of him. No, I inherited a spot of money, to tell you the truth. So, just in case you think I got myself mixed up in some sort of funny business, take it from me, I ain't.'

'Trouble with you chaps is,' Craig said, 'you spend your life lying your heads off, yet, when your stories aren't credited, you whine.'

He was watching Fenley closely. He knew the only way he was going to find out anything, if there was anything to find out, was to goad him into it. Fenley never had been subtle.

'So you don't believe me.'

Fenley sounded extremely hurt. Craig shook his head emphatically.

'All right, Mr. Craig, I'll prove it to yer.' And he slapped a Post Office Savings Book down on the counter under Craig's nose. 'Not only have I picked up the dough honest, I'm putting it away like a good member of the hard-working public.'

Craig eyed him and smiled thinly as he flipped over the pages.

'Managed to put away quite a bit,' he murmured.

The other nodded complacently.

'That's right.'

'Paid in quite a few hundred during the last week, in fact,' went on Craig.

'No law against putting away as much as you wants, so far as I know.'

Craig passed him back his book.

'Well, well,' he told Fenley, 'it all makes a nice change.'

He took Simone's arm, said goodbye to Fenley and left the bar.

Outside she said:

'But he did it, didn't he?'

He grinned at her.

'One of your famous hunches?'

'How will you pin it on him?' she asked.

'Don't let it bother you,' Craig said. 'Fenley has pinned it on himself.'

'What? I didn't notice anything.'

Craig raised an eyebrow. 'You didn't get a chance,' he told her. 'Wait here, just in case he comes out. Follow him.'

She nodded. 'Where are you going?'

'Phone call. Be right back.'

In just under three minutes he returned. Simone was still there and he lit two cigarettes.

'We'll stick around,' he said.

Ten minutes later a large police car drew up at the corner of the mews, out of which two plainclothes men alighted and entered 'The Last Laugh'.

They found Fenley still at the bar, looking as if he'd been there all his life, and they pulled him in.

Twitching slightly, Fenley went with them. He kicked up no sort of fuss at all. Quietly and confidently he told the barman he would be back in half an hour, they hadn't got anything on him.

Outside Craig and Simone saw him into the police car. Fenley eyed Craig sorrowfully and asked whether he thought this was a good sort of turn to do a chap who had gone straight. But he seemed to bear no one any ill will beyond this, merely adding that the whole lot of them were wasting their time, as he would soon show them when he had to answer their questions at the Yard.

In fact, it was quite a shock to him when they took his Post Office Savings Book away from him and indicated a certain page.

Mr. Fenley's language was fluent and remarkable for its vocabulary. When he finally packed it up, he said he was sorry he had forgotten his manners, he was suffering under unusual stress, but he was quite ready to make a statement.

'You see,' Craig explained to Simone over coffee, 'when Fenley got to Wimbledon, he unfortunately found himself short of cash. Quite naturally, he popped into the post office and drew a couple of quid out of his account — forgetting a minor detail, which blew his Brighton alibi to pieces. Still, he's a reasonable character who knows when he's beaten and he'll take it all as part of the game.'

'But the minor detail, what was it?' demanded Simone impatiently.

Craig grinned at her.

'The post office at Wimbledon stamped his precious book with the date and place,' he told her.

11

Beau Brummel and the Blonde

The evening before Craig took a hand in what came to be known as the Beau Brummel Case, P.C. Hall was plodding heavily along the Finchley Road. It had been a hot day and was going to be a hot night and the collar of his uniform was beginning to feel uncomfortably sticky. In addition, his boots hurt him. P.C. Hall was fast coming to the decision there were better jobs than being copper on a beat.

He sighed heavily and turned stolidly off into the quiet little side street. It must be about ten past seven, he always turned that corner about ten past seven. Altogether life was pretty monotonous. He began brooding over the lack of excitement nowadays. Leastways, nothing ever came his way enough to bring him into the limelight and earn recognition

178

from the sergeant. His thoughts broke off as he heard a sudden yell. It was a yell that sent a chill creeping up under P.C. Hall's helmet:

'Help! Help!'

P.C. Hall started to run. His pinching boots were forgotten. Everything obliterated by the outstanding fact that something had happened and *he* wasn't going to be out at the kill. He turned the corner and saw a slightly built man standing out in the middle of the pavement waving his arms and shouting his head off.

'Wot's going on?' puffed P.C. Hall officially.

'Thank God, you're here,' the other gulped hoarsely. 'It's murder.'

'Murder?'

It looked as if P.C. Hall's wish to be in at the kill was due to be answered literally.

'Mr. Delaney. He's up there — on the steps — '

The policeman followed the man up the steps of a large louse. At the top, by the front door which stood wide open, was a crumpled heap. P.C. Hall noticed that the man's head lolled horribly away from his shoulders, and there seemed to him to be blood everywhere.

'Blimey,' he exclaimed, feeling slightly sick. He turned on the little man standing impassively just behind him. 'When — when did this happen? And who are you?'

'My name's Turner. I am — I was — Mr. Delaney's valet. Mr. Delaney had just left the house for a dinner engagement and I heard — '

The other interrupted him to mutter: 'Got to make a report. Telephone.'

Turner's mouth twitched, then he said: 'Inside. In the library.'

P.C. Hall fixed him with an official eye. 'You come in with me,' he said. '*He* won't run away,' he added, refraining from looking at the heap on the top step.

The police didn't take long in coming up to St. John's Wood. They arrived in full force. Police doctor, photograph boys, fingerprint experts. Plus Inspector Holt.

P.C. Hall gave a full report to the Inspector in person. When he had finished, Holt transferred his attention to the valet.

'And you saw nobody?' he queried after he had heard Turner s story.

'No, sir,' the valet answered in his soft voice. 'Except — ' he hesitated. Inspector Holt pounced like a cat on a mouse.

'Except what?'

'Well, sir. As I found Mr. Delaney, I thought I heard the sound of running footsteps. I went out into the street and just as I reached the pavement a man turned the corner I couldn't rightly give a description except that he seemed to be wearing a light suit. He went off in the opposite direction from where the policeman appeared.'

Inspector Holt nodded. There wasn't a hell of a lot to go on, but he'd had less.

'And the servants? You aren't the only member of the household?'

'There is the cook and the butler. Husband and wife. But they are away on holiday at present. Come back Monday. Mr. Delaney had been having most of his meals out, except for his breakfast. I prepared that for him.'

'So at the present there is no one in the house but yourself?'

'No, sir.'

The valet's eyes flickered discreetly. He had learned to be discreet in the service of Carl Delaney.

'A friend of Mr. Delaney,' he said slowly with restraint, 'will want to know what has happened. I ought perhaps to phone. Or had I better wait until the morning sir?'

Inspector Holt looked at him sharply.

'Wait till the morning,' he said. 'They can have the news simultaneously with breakfast.'

'And Mr. Delaney's dinner engagement?'

'You know where he was dining and who with?'

The valet shook his head.

'I have no idea.'

'Then we can't do much about it, can we?' remarked the Inspector irritably. 'This friend you mentioned who — '

They were interrupted by the police doctor. He was proclaiming his opinion that Delaney had died from extensive throat wounds. Inspector Holt's attention was immediately attracted to the doctor's:

'There's a clue for you there too. I should say the blade was drawn from right to left by someone standing behind Delaney. Clean cut, and doesn't look as if there was much of a struggle.'

The Inspector grunted.

'In other words, a left-handed merchant from whom Delaney probably wasn't expecting the attack.'

Presently the police ambulance arrived and departed with the remains of the late Mr. Delaney. The police themselves were the next to depart, leaving a man on duty. They had failed to find the knife.

★   ★   ★

The first inside story Craig heard of the Beau Brummel murder was the following morning, just before lunch. Simone announced a Mrs. Harvey.

She was blonde, if synthetic, and he was well aware of her summing him up through her long thickly mascaraed eyelashes as he bent to light her cigarette.

'So, Mrs. Harvey, what's on your mind?'

She settled her furs round her shoulders — she reminded Craig of a cat stretching itself after a saucer of milk.

'It's a very awkward situation, Mr. Craig.'

He grinned.

'It almost always is,' he told her.

She smiled back at him. Not nervously at all, but a slow, serene smile.

'Yes,' she said, 'but this implicates somebody else. My husband, to be accurate.'

'Tell me more.'

'I don't know whether you know, but a man called Carl Delaney was murdered last night.'

'I saw something about it this morning.'

'He — ' she hesitated. 'He was rather a particular friend of mine. A long time ago, of course.'

'Naturally,' Craig said diplomatically.

The look she flung him was tinged with suspicion and when she spoke there was a challenge in her voice.

'I wrote him several letters.'

Craig nodded understandingly.

'I expect they were slightly foolish,' he

said helpfully. 'What do you want me to do about it?'

She moistened her lips with the tip of her tongue.

'I don't want the police to find them,' she said at last. 'If it isn't too late already. That fool Turner — Carl's valet — didn't phone me until this morning to tell me what had happened and by that time I could read it in the paper.'

'So you came straight round to me.'

She nodded.

'Mrs. Harvey,' he said, 'I am a private eye. Just in case you didn't know, I work with the police.'

There was a short pause, then she said with an edge to her voice:

'I understand all that. But I thought you might — oh, I don't know what to do. Can't you see — ?'

'I think so,' said Craig quietly, but she didn't let him finish.

'All this happened some time ago. It was ended and now — '

'Now,' Craig was ahead of her, 'you're afraid these letters of yours might get your husband mixed up in a murder job?'

'The police will naturally think he had a motive.'

Privately he wondered if she thought her husband had a motive too. Could be, he decided. He tapped the ash off his cigarette.

'I haven't read the full story,' he told her. 'Do you happen to know what time it was when this character Delaney was bumped off?'

'About seven fifteen,' she said promptly.

Craig gave her a long look, then he said:

'Pardon me if I appear nosy, but where were you last night in general and seven fifteen in particular?'

'What d'you mean?'

He grinned at her engagingly.

'Don't get me wrong. If I am going to do anything for you at all, I have to know these little things.'

She relaxed somewhat.

'I suppose you do,' she admitted slowly. 'All right, then, there's no mystery. I was visiting my mother.'

'*With* your husband?'

She threw another sharp glance and

Craig got the impression she was wishing she hadn't come along.

'No,' she said. 'He stayed in. The maid was out and he didn't think we ought to leave the house quite empty with all the burglaries that one reads about going on. But you can't think that he — ?' Her voice tailed off.

Craig treated her to a bleak smile.

'You must admit that it doesn't give him much of an alibi, does it?'

Her reply, when it came, held a note of despair.

'Then you won't help me?'

'I didn't say that. For a fee I will undertake to see how the land lies. But, don't let's make any mistake about it, this is a case of murder.'

'Of course, I understand perfectly,' she told him in a low voice.

He stood up.

'I'll do what I can. If you leave your address with my secretary, I'll be getting in touch with you.'

He put his feet up on the desk after she had gone and smoked a cigarette through. He had to turn things over in his mind, and he was trying to recall all he had ever known of Carl Delaney, the man whose friends styled Beau Brummel. Presently, he picked up his hat and went through into the outer office.

'Did you catch all that glamour on the way out?' he asked Simone.

She smiled at him.

'I couldn't miss.'

'I've got a call to make,' he said. 'I'll pick you up here in about an hour. I've a feeling we might be paying a visit to St. John's Wood.'

He got a taxi outside and rattled off in the direction of Scotland Yard. He found his old friend Inspector Holt behind his blackened, bubbling pipe, frowning over a letter.

'Huh?' grunted Holt.

'Busy?' asked Craig laconically.

Holt looked round his paper-littered desk, and grimaced.

'Nice juicy little case of murder. Read about it?'

'Carl Delaney?'

The Inspector replaced his pipe between his teeth.

'Got quite a write-up this morning, without giving many of the facts away, either. Not that there are many to go on,' he added bitterly.

Craig didn't take a lot of notice of this. Inspector Holt always described his cases that way. They never had many facts. It was a matter of pride with him.

'Heard of him,' he was saying.

'Delaney?'

Craig nodded:

'Best-dressed man in town. With an eye for curves and knowing all the angles.'

The Inspector looked at him solemnly. 'You make him sound like a geometrical expert,' he said. 'Which I understand, wasn't quite his hobby. But that's him. Beau Brummel, twentieth century edition.'

Craig said, 'What happened?'

The Inspector started using up matches on his pipe.

'Found on the steps of his house by his valet yesterday evening — with his throat cut,' he grunted between puffs.

'Messy.'

'I'll say. And he was wearing the very

smartest dinner jacket I've seen in years,' he added. 'Quite ruined it was. Tck, tck,' he sighed exaggeratedly.

Craig grinned. He queried:

'What's the valet's story?'

The Inspector shrugged.

'Straightforward enough. Name of Turner, and he told us Delaney was leaving for a dinner engagement just before seven fifteen. Turner apparently heard a scream almost immediately after the front door shut, and whipped downstairs. When he got out there he found Delaney lying in a pool of blood at the top of the steps. Seemed quite a cold-blooded fish about the whole thing.'

'Anything else?'

'Turner said he saw someone running down the street. Couldn't identify him though, so it was probably just one of those things. Anyway, it's not much of a lead. He yelled for help and a policeman on his beat came running.'

Craig flicked a flame into life from his lighter.

'You found the knife?'

The Inspector shook his head regretfully.

'Murderer probably took it with him.'

'Then you think something of the valet's story about somebody running away?'

'I'm keeping an open mind. We have got a clue from the wound though. The blade was drawn from right to left by somebody standing behind Delaney.' He eyed Craig keenly as he spoke.

Craig didn't disappoint him.

'Left-handed character, eh?'

'There was a bloody fingerprint on Delaney's white tie too. But too blurred for identification.'

Craig took a deep drag at his cigarette. 'Delaney have any visitors before he left the house?'

Inspector Holt shook his head slowly.

'Apparently not. Valet was with him for the best part of an hour, and then saw him go downstairs. That was the last time he saw him alive. There are no other servants in the house at present.'

Craig leaned forward and nodded towards the sheet of paper the other had before him. 'What about that you were reading?'

The Inspector picked it up and threw it over to Craig.

'It was found on Delaney at the mortuary,' he said tersely. 'Apparently he'd been running round with a Mrs. Harvey some time or another. Hubby got wind of it and maybe this is the result. The letter threatened Carl with all sorts of nasty things if he didn't keep off the grass. We've asked Harvey to look in and have a chat.'

Craig grinned at him through a cloud of cigarette smoke.

'Come on, give — you've got something else on your master-mind.'

'Damn you,' Holt grumbled good-humouredly. 'I just think Harvey might — well, like I said, I'm keeping an open mind. But the valet wanted to phone somebody last night to let them know about Delaney. I have found out since it was Mrs. Harvey.'

'You don't say,' drawled Craig.

Holt glared at him, a slightly puzzled expression appearing on his face. He started to say something, then a policeman came in accompanied by a heavily built man of uncertain age with greying hair. Craig eyed the newcomer and wondered why Mrs. Harvey had ever said 'Yes'.

Inspector Holt was saying smoothly:

'I'm sorry to bother you like this, Mr. Harvey, but I should like to know one or two little details in connection with the death of Carl Delaney last night.'

'I don't know anything about it and if you think — '

Holt picked up the letter Craig had replaced on the desk.

'For instance,' he said quietly, 'can you identify this?'

Harvey glanced at it and said belligerently:

'I wrote it, if that's what you mean.'

'That's what I mean. Wouldn't write with your left hand by any chance?'

The other stared at him.

'What are you getting at?'

'Are you, or are you not, left-handed?' the Inspector persisted.

'I am. What of it?'

'Only,' said Inspector Holt gently, 'that Delaney was killed by a left-handed man.'

'May I point out,' Harvey said heavily, 'that there are plenty of left-handed men in the world besides myself.'

The Inspector shook his head sadly.

'That's what makes it so difficult for me, Mr. Harvey.'

'As for that,' Harvey pointed a scornful finger at the letter, 'I am well aware it puts me in a spot, but it doesn't prove anything at all.'

The Inspector looked at him. 'It might help,' he said.

Craig stood up.

'I must be getting along,' he said easily. 'My secretary will be worried about me, especially if she guesses where I am.'

★   ★   ★

Craig kept the taxi waiting outside his office while he waited for Simone. She came down at a run, cramming her hat onto the back of her head.

'Did you get on to anything?' she inquired breathlessly as they got into the taxi.

'Case would look pretty black against blonde-and-beautiful's hubby. But Holt knows he hasn't got enough evidence to convict a mouse. Still, he's only just beginning. Anyway, I thought we'd look in at the scene of the crime — just for the hell of it.'

A slight little man with light-coloured hair opened the door to them.

'I thought the police had everything in hand?' he objected when Craig told him who he was.

'You would be the valet, Turner. I've just left Inspector Holt. If we came in,' Craig said, smiling bleakly, 'it would be a lot easier to talk.'

The other didn't look exactly overwhelmed with joy at the prospect of a chat, Craig thought. But he never had been one to be too over-sensitive about his fellow creatures' emotional reactions.

'Thanks,' he said. The valet stood aside. They went through the large hall into a pleasant room in the front of the house.

Turner's bird-like face was perfectly impassive but he fingered his tie with nervous fingers. Craig noticed how large his hands appeared.

The little man spoke:
'I have told the police all I know. I am

afraid it is quite useless coming to me for further information.'

'I know you spilled quite a yarn.' Craig gazed at him coolly. 'But I thought you might care to give me something different.'

The other's face didn't move a muscle.

'I'm sorry, sir, I don't understand exactly what you mean.'

Craig said:

'I want the true story. Is that in short enough words for you?'

'True story, sir?'

Simone could have sworn that the valet's air of utter bafflement was genuine. But Craig continued with remorseless affability:

'You know. The one about how you killed your boss. And the reason, and all that.'

Turner recoiled as if somebody had kicked him in the pit of his stomach. There was no air of bewilderment about him now.

'What do you know?' he said softly, menace in his voice.

'I know, for instance,' Craig said easily

'that Carl Delaney must have been killed in the house, by somebody he never would have suspected. I know he must have been dressed *after* he was dead and then dumped on the steps.'

Turner, who had been gazing at him in a mesmerized fashion, suddenly lunged violently but unscientifically, with the result that his chin encountered Craig's fist with considerable force. The next moment he was sprawled on the carpet, out cold.

He was still out when the police arrived.

Back in the office, Simone declared:

'What a horrible business. Carl Delaney finds out he had stolen money from him, gives him the chance of returning it instead of informing the police — and Turner kills him.'

Craig nodded and said:

'Turner thought he could pin it on somebody else with the aid of Harvey's letter. He was very careful to tell Mrs. H. of what had happened, and very careful to tip off the cops delicately, of course, about Mrs. H. Still,' he went on, 'Turner must have been badly rattled when he'd done the job to have made that one stupid slip.'

'Which was?' Simone asked him dutifully.

He grinned at her.

'For a valet, it was extremely careless to dress Beau Brummel Delaney up in a white tie and dinner jacket. *White ties go with tails*.' He grinned at her.

She liked the way he grinned at her.

'Remind me to show you sometime,' he said.

12

The Hampstead Kidnapping

Craig, leaning on the bell-push of the big house in Hampstead waiting for someone to answer his ring, idly wondered why he felt so impatient. He decided that this time of the evening everybody was in a hurry. Going home. Going to meet a date. Into his reverie broke the butler's voice:

'Yes, sir?'

The man was tall and dark with black crinkly hair and a clean-shaven face. There was something oddly familiar about that face, Craig thought. He gave up trying to place him to say, 'Mr. Belmont's expecting me.'

'What name, sir?'

Craig told him his name and continued to scrutinize the butler's face. There was not a trace of emotion there. Craig decided he must have been mistaken in thinking he had seen him before.

The butler was leading the way across the hall. Craig followed him into the study and Belmont got up to greet him. He was a middle-aged man, and he was wearing an anxious and harassed expression above his neat bow tie.

'Good evening, Mr. Craig.' He twirled a pair of horn-rimmed glasses between nervy fingers. 'You must be wondering why I called you so urgently on the phone,' he went on. 'I'm afraid I sounded very incoherent and hysterical, but I have had a great shock.'

'You said it was your wife who'd had the shock,' Craig reminded him.

'Yes, yes. And now you're here I expect you will tell me it was the police I ought to have called in.'

Craig raised an interrogative eyebrow.

'All I got on the phone,' he said, 'was that your wife was passing out. Suppose you tell me more?'

'It is our little boy. He has disappeared. Kidnapped.'

'What time was this?'

'About half past five. Just before I phoned you.'

'Why *didn't* you call the police?'

There was a slight pause, before the other began:

'I — I should explain — ' He hesitated again. Then: 'My wife is neurotic. It's my own fault. I've spoilt her. Ever since our marriage I've let her have her own way too much. And now — well — I'm reaping the benefits.' Craig had been wondering what that harassed expression stood for. Now he knew.

He watched the other light a cigarette with a shaky hand. Belmont said:

'Lately she's developed a kind of persecution complex.'

Craig cut in with: 'How about the child? How does he fit into all this?'

Again that hesitation. Belmont answered at last:

'My wife felt that he had come between us. It isn't true, of course, but it made everything very difficult.'

Craig nodded, turning to stare out of the window into the darkness that was beginning to creep slowly over the Heath. He looked at Belmont and suggested:

'Can I see your wife?'

'Certainly. She is in her room lying down, but she will see you. Will you come with me?'

As they went out into the hall, Belmont called after the figure of the butler who was just emerging from the dining room.

'Yelton.'

The man stopped and turned quickly.

'Yes, sir?'

'If the telephone should ring I shall be upstairs with Mrs. Belmont. Let me know at once.'

'Very good, sir.'

A woman's voice, low and caught up in undertones of tragedy, answered Belmont's knock. Craig followed Belmont in.

It was exactly the sort of room Craig had imagined the sort of woman he had expected Mrs. Belmont to be would have. Everything laid on with a trowel. A fitted carpet in which he sank to his ankles, velvet hangings, smothering luxurious bed and Mrs. Belmont herself, reclining with her head propped up by half a dozen cushions, and her pale oval face revealed by discreet lighting. Craig put her down as thirty-five. Her mouth was petulant and drooping above a stubborn chin.

She gave Craig a fleeting glance and then looked beyond him.

'Who's this?' she asked her husband.

He introduced them in a tired voice.

The woman's large eyes came back to rest on Craig.

'You don't look like a detective.'

He grinned at her engagingly and quirked an eyebrow.

'Maybe I should have kept my hat on,' he said.

She managed a flickering smile.

'I'm so tired, Mr. Craig, and now this tragedy has come to the house, I — '

Her voice tailed off artistically. Every inflection in her speech was studied, Craig thought.

A tap at the door and it was the manservant.

'Dr. Fowler is on the telephone, sir.'

'Thank you, Yelton. I'll come at once.'

At the door he said to Craig:

'My wife will explain to you what happened.'

'Tell the doctor I need something for my nerves. I don't feel as if 1 shall ever sleep again,' the woman called after him.

'Yes, my dear.'

Belmont went out, closing the door softly behind him.

There was a little silence while Mrs. Belmont stared at Craig with a speculative look in her eyes. Craig waited for her to start things going.

After a few moments she said, her voice sharp:

'Aren't you going to do something?'

Craig smiled: 'Before I do something, I'll have to know something.'

'Questions, questions,' she exclaimed tragically. 'All right. What is it you want to know? But I should have thought my husband could have answered your questions just as well.'

'At the moment he's telling your doctor your nerves are giving you hell,' he told her. He went on, 'Would there have been a nursemaid around at the time your child was kidnapped?'

The woman frowned petulantly.

'I dismissed her this morning,' she said. 'She was having a bad influence on the child. I never liked her. I would never have engaged her in the first place, but I was overruled by my husband.'

Craig privately wondered if Belmont had ever overruled his wife in all their life together. He said: 'You suspect her of being involved?'

'I don't know. She might be.'

Craig tried another angle.

'When did you last see the kid?'

'I left him in the nursery after I had given him his tea.' Her voice rose hysterically. 'Don't ask me all these questions. Questions, questions — I can't bear it any more!'

Craig told her coolly:

'I'm trying to find out, Mrs. Belmont, when you first discovered the kid had gone.'

'I went to my room then I went back to the nursery. I suppose it was about half an hour after I had left Gerald. And — and he wasn't there. I found this note.'

Mrs. Belmont picked up a folded piece of paper that lay on the bedside table. She handed it to Craig. It was rough copybook paper with a torn edge. On it was a printed message:

'WE 'AVE TOOK YORE LITTEL BOY. FIVE 'UNDRED WILL GET 'IM BACK. WE'LL PHONE YOU TONITE AND TELL YOU WERE TO SEND THE MONEY. KEEP YORE MOUTH SHUT AND DO WOT WE SAY.'

Craig looked at the note again, then at her. 'I'm sure it must have been grim for you — '

'It was terrible. Terrible. My poor child — '

Craig raised an ironical eyebrow. 'You were pretty fond of him?'

'He is all I've got in the world,' she told him passionately.

Craig looked at her bleakly. 'Wonder what your husband would say to that? But maybe that wouldn't be getting us anywhere, anyway.'

The woman made no reply, but sank back again on her pillows as her husband returned. Belmont took one look at his wife then threw an apprehensive glance at Craig. But there was inquiry in his eyes as well.

Craig caught the look and smiled.

'Is the doctor fixing up some sleeping

tablets for your wife?' he asked. 'She may need them.'

'Why — ?'

'What do you mean?' The woman sat up suddenly.

'It's all right,' Craig reassured Belmont, then turned to the other, whose exclamation held an underlying hint of fear. 'Your kid's safe enough.' Back to Belmont: 'And if your wife will only be her age and tell us where he is — '

'What?' Belmont snapped, shooting a glance at the woman, then back to Craig. Mrs. Belmont said:

'What are you saying?'

Craig tapped the note he held. 'You wrote this — to yourself.'

Looking as if he'd been hit by a chunk of rock, Belmont stepped forward. 'But I don't understand — ?'

'Mrs. Belmont does.' Craig turned to the woman. 'Overdid it a bit, though, didn't you? No one who was as illiterate as this indicates would put in apostrophes where they had dropped aitches.'

She sat up, staring at him with hatred in her eyes. 'Don't listen to him,' she flung at her husband.

Craig went on relentlessly:

'She roped in your manservant and dreamed up a neurotic little notion of scoring off you for getting too fond of your son and at the same time grabbing back your sympathy and loving attention.'

'Lies!' shouted Mrs. Belmont.

Belmont looked from one to the other, then:

'I am becoming rather interested,' he told Craig quietly. 'Go on.'

'You can't stand there and say these things,' raged the woman. 'You can't prove anything!'

Craig smiled at her cynically.

'When somebody starts in telling me I can't prove anything, it means I've been right all along.' He turned to the man. 'You tipped me off when you called your manservant by the name Yelton.' To the woman he went on, 'You threatened to expose him as a jailbird if he didn't help you in your little game.'

Mrs. Belmont caved in. She went off into a mild fit of hysterics, then sobbed wildly into the pillows.

'*Where is Gerald?*'

She looked up and told Belmont, tears streaming down her face:

'Notley took him to the nurse's house. The nurse who left this morning. He's all right.'

She went off into another paroxysm of weeping. The other turned away. 'Come along,' he said wearily to Craig, 'she'll calm down if we leave her.'

As Belmont handed Craig a cheque and replaced the cap on his fountain pen, he remarked:

'I shan't bring any charge against the manservant. How did you know his real name is Notley by the way?'

'The last time I saw him,' said Craig reminiscently, 'was in the dock just before he collected a stretch for kidnapping. He wore a heavy moustache then, and his hair wasn't dyed black. It was that fooled me at first. Until you called him Yelton. Then the penny dropped. After that, tying up the note with her knowledge of his identity, it was easy to guess what had happened. You see,' he said, 'Yelton is Notley, spelt backwards.'

13

The Menaced Eccentric

Craig's clients made a pretty varied collection. Young, wealthy women who were getting themselves blackmailed; wealthier men or women who had the jitters over the safety of their precious family heirlooms. And occasionally just to make a change, members of the ex-crook class appealed to him for help. Taken all in all, Craig fancied he had quite a psychological slant on characters from every walk of life.

But there came a day when a rarer specimen walked into the office. Naturally, with a name like Theodore Penrose, he had to be slightly on the eccentric side.

His office door stealthily eased open a crack and as Craig eyed it with some curiosity, a large moustache appeared.

'Mr. Craig?' the moustache asked.

The moustache, followed by its owner,

neatly clad in sober navy-blue, advanced slowly. Craig began to regret Simone had slipped out on a routine job. He needed Simone around to protect him from this sort of intrusion.

The newcomer, peering short-sightedly over its moustache, placed his bowler hat tidily on the desk and leaned forward at a precarious angle on his rolled umbrella.

'I wanted to see you,' he began tentatively.

'I'll try and keep still and make it easy for you.'

The other said, 'You see, Mr. Craig, I am going to be murdered.'

'Really? Why?'

'I don't know. I don't know, at all.'

'Who are you?' Craig said. 'And who wants to blot you out?'

'My name is Theodore Penrose. I'm afraid I don't know who would do such a thing, but the fact remains.'

'No?' Craig was beginning to wonder if he was still in his own office or had wandered into a crazier kind of nightmare.

'If I had known,' went on Theodore Penrose, 'I should have gone to the police and lodged my complaint.' He pursed his lips and proceeded. 'However, I felt if I went to them with my story as it stands, they might think I was imagining things. Which is why I have come to you. I do hope you are not very expensive.'

Craig said he hoped he wasn't all that expensive. 'And how does your story stand at the moment?' he said. He had a feeling any story Theodore Penrose dreamed up might switch this way, that way, as and when.

'Every night for the last two weeks,' the other was saying, 'a man's voice has telephoned me and told me my life was in danger. In the nature of a warning, you understand?'

Craig said he thought he understood.

'And then, last night, I'm sure I heard mysterious footsteps outside my house after dark. What do you make of that?'

Craig thought he could make practically anything of it, but he didn't say so. Instead he said:

'Was it always the same voice phoned you?'

The other nodded emphatically.

'Sometimes I thought it was disguised. But I am not a fool.'

Craig told him he was sure he wasn't. 'Could it be you have some money tucked in the old tea caddy?'

A shadow of surprise crossed Theodore Penrose's face, and the moustache wavered uncertainly. 'I do keep a certain amount of money on the premises. In the event of an emergency I feel it is needful. Not, however, in the tea caddy. Why?'

'Motive.'

The other blinked at him short-sightedly. 'Yes, I see.' He thought about it for a moment, then something occurred to him. He said slowly, 'But who would know? I live alone, Mr. Craig, quite alone.'

Craig regarded him thoughtfully.

Privately, he decided Theodore Penrose was just a tight-fisted little eccentric who had got a pretty thick wad hoarded up in his house and was beginning to develop a complex about it being pinched.

'My advice,' Craig said at last, 'is go to the police. They stand a much better chance of digging out this character who's annoying you and putting the lid on him.'

Theodore Penrose regarded him silently for a minute. Then he said:

'I'm very much afraid, Mr. Craig, that you do not take me seriously. However, I thank you for your advice. If I have any further annoyance, I shall consider acting upon it.'

He clasped his bowler hat firmly and made his way to the door. He turned and said:

'In case you should change your mind and would care to investigate the trouble — for a not too prohibitive fee, of course — I will leave you my address and telephone number.'

He fished in his waistcoat pocket, took out a small piece of pasteboard, and brought it solemnly over to the desk.

'Good day to you,' he said, and sidled out.

Craig glanced at the Theodore Penrose address. It was in St. John's Wood. The more he stared the more a thought grew in the back of his mind, until he picked up the telephone and dialled a number.

Later that day, Craig found the small, semi-detached villa in a little street off St.

John's Wood Road. It was badly in need of a coat of paint and altogether exceedingly dismal-looking and thoroughly dreary. The gate squeaked as Craig made his way up the short conventional garden path. A postman was a little ahead of him, banging with a subdued violence on the front door knocker.

Craig queried:

'What's up?'

'Dunno. Can't get no answer. Don't seem to be nobody at home. I got this to deliver.'

He twisted the registered package in his hand over.

'Door is open,' Craig said.

The other nodded thoughtfully.

'And that's queer too. Not like Mr. Penrose, it ain't, to go out and leave the door on the jar.'

Craig pushed the door wide and called:

'Any one at home?'

There was no reply.

'Whassat?' the postman gulped suddenly.

Somewhere from the darkness of the hall came a stifled groan. Craig was through the door and into the front room, with the postman at his heels.

'Cor!' The postman stared at Theodore Penrose lying in a crumpled heap on the floor. 'Looks like he's had it.'

Craig bent quickly. The unconscious man's pulse was very faint, but at least he was alive.

They managed to get him fairly comfortable and Craig went back into the hall in search of a telephone. He phoned the police and a doctor, and returned to find the postman eyeing a heavy brass candlestick, which lay on the carpet.

'That's wot he done it with,' the postman deduced. 'Real nasty, I calls it.'

Craig too eyed the candlestick. Then his attention was attracted by something else. He picked it up, turning the object over and over in his hand. His gaze travelled round the meagrely furnished room. He wondered why anyone decently well-off should deliberately choose to live the life of a comparative pauper. Into his speculations rang a shrill summons from the doorbell.

'Doctor or cops,' said the postman,

cocking his head on one side.

But it was a short tubby little man with a tanned face, looking a clean-shaven and healthier edition of Theodore Penrose. He was Penrose's brother, he said.

'Come in,' Craig said. 'You're just in time.'

'In time — ?' The newcomer gave Craig a puzzled look, but followed him into the front room.

'Good Heavens! What's happened?'

'Someone took a dislike to your brother.'

'Is he — ?'

'I think he'll live,' Craig told him.

The other (his name was Herbert Penrose) looked at Craig. 'But — who on earth would want to kill him?'

Craig raised an eyebrow.

'For his money maybe?'

Herbert Penrose glanced round the room. 'It doesn't look as if that could be the reason.'

'No?' Craig drawled. 'You didn't know he was the thrifty type, who hid it away in an old sock?'

Well — ' the other hesitated. 'Poor old

Theo was always a bit funny. Eccentric, you know. But I haven't seen him for several years. I've been abroad. Australia. I only got back to the old country today, and I came straight here.' He looked back at the still figure on the couch and shook his head sadly. 'Never thought I'd find him this way, though.'

Craig was busy lighting a cigarette.

'He wasn't expecting you? Cigarette?'

'Thanks. I could do with one.'

Herbert Penrose took the proffered cigarette and fumbled for a match. Craig gave him a light from his lighter.

Herbert Penrose shook his head. 'I'm afraid we'd rather lost touch. Bit of a rolling stone, I am, you see. I just thought I'd give him a surprise.'

He swung round as there came a second ring at the doorbell. Two plain-clothes men and the doctor had arrived at one and the same time.

'In here,' Craig told them. The doctor made his way straight over to the couch, and after a few minutes disentangled himself from his stethoscope and said:

'He'll pull through all right.' He turned

to the police officers. 'We must get him to hospital.'

One of them volunteered. 'I'll phone through.'

'Phone's in the hall,' Craig said.

Herbert Penrose was frowning anxiously. He turned to the doctor. 'Will he be all right? Will he live?'

It was Craig who answered him, so quietly it was almost casual. 'The doctor has already said he will.' He went on smoothly: 'Altogether, you didn't make much of a job of it, did you?'

Herbert Penrose goggled at him.

'I didn't — I don't know what you're driving at.'

'Perhaps this will refresh your memory.'

Craig held out a small object in his hand.

The other recoiled as if Craig had been holding a cobra. 'Where did you find that?' he whispered.

'Let me tell you a little story.' Craig included the doctor, the postman and the plainclothes man in his grin. 'Once upon a time there was a wicked brother called Herbert. He came back home from

Australia, where he'd been for some years. When he arrived he thought it would be fun to scare the daylights out of his elder brother, Theodore. He spent a whole two weeks doing this by giving him ghostly warnings down the telephone in a disguised voice. That way, he figured, when the police eventually caught up with what was going on, suspicion would be thrown on to what is technically known as person or persons unknown. Next, Herbert decided it was time to finish the game, so he drops in here, dots his brother one with a candlestick and departs with the money Theodore had been hiding away for a rainy day. After that, Herbert thought he was sitting pretty, until he suddenly remembered something he had left behind. It was pretty damning evidence, so there was only one thing left for him to do — go right back and fetch it. Unfortunately for wicked brother Herbert, it had already been found.'

Craig broke off and glanced at Herbert Penrose whose face was ashen.

'Here,' he said and the other caught the object thrown him, 'that's what you left behind.' He went on: 'I checked up a

Herbert Penrose arrived from Australia *two weeks ago*, which fits in nicely with the phone calls Theodore Penrose had been receiving. I knew you were him all right when you walked in. Our summers don't run to the sun tan you're wearing.'

The plainclothes man moved in on Herbert Penrose.

'Have you anything to say?'

The other made no reply. He could only stare fixedly down at the lighter that glinted up from his palm. A nice lighter it was. With clearly cut initials: 'H.P.' and underneath in smaller lettering but just as clear: 'Made in Australia'.

14

The Lawyer and the Blonde

'We're our way to see a lawyer,' Craig told Simone as their taxi turned off Oxford Street.

'Who is in trouble?' she asked in her attractive French accent.

Craig grinned.

'He is,' he said. 'If you can tell by the tone of a voice over the telephone.'

He went on to explain to her how the lawyer, Turnell, had asked him to come over as there was something worrying him, but Craig had been held up at his office. He'd told Turnell he'd get over just as soon as he could make it.

The taxi pulled up outside a block of flats in Mayfair. Simone remarked:

'He must be a rather expensive lawyer.'

Craig nodded. It was one of those small blocks of flats with a very exclusive atmosphere that set the tenants back plenty just to breathe it.

A lift took them swiftly to the third floor and Turnell's flat. Craig rang and, as the door was flung open, he walked straight into the arms of a slim blonde.

Simone thought Craig took longer than was really necessary to break the clinch. The woman at the door was beautiful, with hair to her shoulders and slanting violet eyes.

The blonde spoke first. She said:

'I'm so sorry.'

'Think nothing of it,' Craig smiled.

She was staring at him uncertainly. She glanced from him to Simone, who smiled at her without meaning it one little bit. The blonde swung back to Craig. She said:

'I don't know who you are, but if you have come to see my brother, I — I think you had better leave.'

Craig edged himself into the hall and told her pleasantly:

'I'm here to see Mr. Turnell.'

The woman closed the door and paused hesitantly. She told Craig:

'I'm Miss Turnell. I'm afraid my

brother's dead. It's — it's suicide.'

Craig didn't bat an eyelash.

'When?' he asked.

They were in the large sitting room, luxuriously furnished, with tall French windows that opened onto a low balcony overlooking the square. Simone thought it was a lovely room with a charming view. The woman was saying:

'Just — just before you arrived.' There was a movement at the door and she turned and said, 'This is Mr. Manville, my brother's clerk.'

A little man with a thin pointed face and sleek black hair came into the room. The blonde suddenly slumped into a chair. Craig thought she had very nice legs. She looked up at him. Her voice cracked on a sob and she lowered her eyes as she said:

'This has been a terrible shock.'

For the first time the little man spoke. Turning from the blonde, he said to Craig:

'May I ask who you are?'

Craig told him and said he had an appointment with Turnell. The blonde's eyes widened. Craig said to her:

'Suppose you tell me what happened before I take a look at the body?'

'He has been very nervy lately — he suffered rather badly from insomnia. I've been trying to persuade him to see a doctor. You see, I — I was afraid something like this might happen.'

'If you were that psychic, why didn't you try and do something about it?' Craig asked her.

'You don't know my brother — he wouldn't ever listen to advice.'

'That's true enough,' the thin-faced man put in.

The woman went on in a low voice:

'He didn't go to the office this morning. I had a hairdressing appointment and when I returned Mr. Manville came out of the bedroom and told me my brother had gassed himself.'

Craig turned to Manville.

'Maybe you could add something to this?' he said.

'It was as Miss Turnell says,' the other gulped. 'I called with some papers for signature. There was no one in. When I saw what had happened, I turned off the gas and opened all the windows. I heard Miss Turnell arrive and I came out. I told her, then afterwards you came.'

Craig took out his cigarette case. His gaze flickered to the blonde. He said:

'Had your brother anything on his mind?'

'Only not being able to sleep and worrying about his health.'

Craig eyed her thoughtfully over the flame of his lighter. Then, as he applied the flame to his cigarette, he murmured:

'Wonder why he wanted to see me? I'm not a doctor exactly.'

'He must have had something on his mind that he did not want to tell me about.'

'He must have,' Craig said. To Manville: 'I want to see him.' Then to the woman: 'How about any servants?'

'There was a maid,' she said, 'but I had to sack her yesterday.'

'Too bad.'

The clerk led the way to the bedroom. As he was about to open the door, Craig said:

'Did he leave you any farewell message?'

She started to shake her head when Manville cut in:

'I believe he did.' She shot him a look. 'I didn't tell you,' he went on quickly. 'I — I thought I saw a sheet of paper on the table.'

'What's it say?' Craig asked.

'Frankly,' the other muttered, 'I was too shocked to look.'

There were French windows in this room and they, too, opened on to a low balcony overlooking the square. The windows were wide open and the gas had almost dispersed. Craig went in, followed by Simone. The blonde and the little man framed themselves in the doorway. Turnell lay on his face in front of an ornate gas fire. He was a large, thick-set shape in pyjamas and an ornate dressing-gown. Craig looked him over. He was dead all right.

Craig moved over and picked up a typewritten sheet of notepaper on the bedside table. He noticed a portable typewriter in the corner of the room. He read the message thoughtfully, then said:

'This your brother's signature?'

He took the notepaper over, folding it so that only the scrawled signature was visible, and showed it to the girl.

'Y — yes,' she choked. 'What does he say?'

Craig grinned at her slowly.

'He says he leaves ten thousand to his clerk — '

'What — !' Her voice was a sudden screech. 'It isn't true — '

Craig slewed round to Manville.

'Lucky, aren't you?' he told him. Before the other could answer, the blonde was screaming at him:

'You rat! It's murder, that's what it is — you killed him!' She turned to Craig. 'Don't you see it's murder?' she yelled. 'My brother would never have written a note like that — '

Craig raised an eyebrow.

'You really think not?' His tone was edged with sarcasm. 'And how — just as a matter of interest — would you know?'

'Well — I — ' She bit her lip. 'Never mind, I just know. What are you waiting for?'

Manville was very white, but his thin features twisted in a smile.

'You don't know what you're talking about,' he told her. 'You never got on with your brother — '

'You double-crosser,' she choked. 'You think you can pull that on me — I'll see you damned first — '

Craig tapped the note impatiently and broke in:

'Suppose you cut the comedy cross-talk and take it easy until the police arrive?'

She swung on him, her hair falling over one eye. He heard a muttered exclamation and turned as Manville made a sudden move. He jerked his head back and the breeze of the other's vicious fist fanned his cheek. Craig pivoted and almost nonchalantly sank a dig into Manville's stomach, doubling him up like a hairpin.

'Any lawyer,' he told the blonde casually, glancing up at her from Manville, 'knows a bequest in a mere note, unwitnessed at that, would be completely invalid. Just a little legal point Manville tripped up on. Incidentally,' he murmured, 'I'd be interested to know how he got into the flat with no one to answer the door. Or did you lend him your key?'

She looked as if he'd struck her across the face.

'Why you — !' and then she was struggling with Simone who held her arm twisted behind her back.

'Very nice,' grinned Craig at Simone. 'I'll take over while you call the police.'

He held the blonde in a grip that held her writhing but powerless, and Simone picked up the telephone.

Later, on the way home in a taxi, Craig said:

'Manville was crazy about her, and she played him for the mug she thought he was. She got him in to fix her brother, promising him a cut of the cash she'd collect.'

Simone nodded.

'She looked the sort who went in for twisting infatuated men round her little finger,' she said.

'Then, at the last minute,' Craig went on, 'he suddenly realized he was being played for a chump and he got a different idea. He forged the note and planted it there behind her back. He never imagined she'd have the nerve to turn on him the way she did.'

Simone smiled at him admiringly.

'Perhaps some day,' she sighed, shaking her head, 'I shall catch on as quickly as you do — '

The taxi gave a sudden swerve and threw her against him. Her arms went round his neck.

'From where I'm sitting,' he grinned at her, 'you're not doing so badly right now.'

THE END